DREAMS
with FAITH

Holiday Dreams Book 2
A Sweet Historical Western Romance
by
USA TODAY Bestselling Author
SHANNA HATFIELD

Dreams With Faith
Holiday Dreams Book 2

Copyright © 2024 by Shanna Hatfield

ISBN: 9798320907277

All rights reserved. No part of this publication may be reproduced, distributed, downloaded, decompiled, reverse engineered, transmitted, or stored in or introduced into any information storage and retrieval system, in any form or by any means, including photocopying, recording, or other electronic or mechanical methods, now known or hereafter invented, without the written permission of the author, except in the case of brief quotations embodied in reviews and certain other noncommercial uses permitted by copyright law. Please purchase only authorized editions.

For permission requests, please contact the author, with a subject line of "permission request" at the email address below or through her website.

Shanna Hatfield
shanna@shannahatfield.com

This is a work of fiction. Names, characters, businesses, places, events, and incidents either are the product of the author's imagination or are used in a fictitious manner. Any resemblance to actual persons, living or dead, business establishments, or actual events is purely coincidental.

Published by Wholesome Hearts Publishing, LLC.
wholesomeheartspublishing@gmail.com

Dedication

*To those who dream
with faith in their hearts.*

Books by Shanna Hatfield

FICTION

CONTEMPORARY

Holiday Brides
Valentine Bride
Summer Bride
Easter Bride
Lilac Bride
Lake Bride

Rodeo Romance
The Christmas Cowboy
Wrestling Christmas
Capturing Christmas
Barreling Through Christmas
Chasing Christmas
Racing Christmas
Keeping Christmas
Roping Christmas
Remembering Christmas
Savoring Christmas
Taming Christmas
Tricking Christmas

Grass Valley Cowboys
The Cowboy's Christmas Plan
The Cowboy's Spring Romance
The Cowboy's Summer Love
The Cowboy's Autumn Fall
The Cowboy's New Heart
The Cowboy's Last Goodbye

Summer Creek
Catching the Cowboy
Rescuing the Rancher
Protecting the Princess
Distracting the Deputy
Guiding the Grinch
Challenging the Chef

HISTORICAL

Pendleton Petticoats
Dacey   Bertie
Aundy   Millie
Caterina   Dally
Ilsa   Quinn
Marnie   Evie
Lacey   Sadie

Baker City Brides
Crumpets and Cowpies
Thimbles and Thistles
Corsets and Cuffs
Bobbins and Boots
Lightning and Lawmen
Dumplings and Dynamite

Hearts of the War
Garden of Her Heart
Home of Her Heart
Dream of Her Heart

Hardman Holidays
The Christmas Bargain
The Christmas Token
The Christmas Calamity
The Christmas Vow
The Christmas Quandary
The Christmas Confection
The Christmas Melody
The Christmas Ring
The Christmas Wish
The Christmas Kiss

Holiday Express
Holiday Hope
Holiday Heart
Holiday Home
Holiday Love

Chapter One

January 1886
Altoona, Pennsylvania

"Is there a particular reason you're trying to stir up a heap of trouble, little sister?"

Keeva Holt glanced over her shoulder at her brother. She might have stuck her tongue out at Davin, but his firm grip on the back of her coat was the only thing keeping her from toppling out of the sleigh her father drove down the curving hillside road to the church. She leaned a little farther out, draped her purple scarf over the corner post of Mr. Lubbock's fence, then plopped back into her seat.

As she adjusted her skirts, she cast another look at Davin. "I'm not stirring up trouble, just offering an incentive."

"An incentive!" Davin nearly shouted, drawing the gazes of both their parents. "It's not an incentive, Keeva. You might as well race up to a bee's nest and give it a good kick while you're at it."

"I might if it weren't snowing!" Keeva tamped down the urge to smack Davin with her gloves. Just because he was older, he seemed to think that entitled him to boss her around. She'd be eighteen at the end of March, and then she'd be all grown up, beyond anyone telling her what to do.

"What's going on back there?" their mother asked. Eira Holt was a force to be reckoned with on a good day, and Keeva had no desire to stir her mother's wrath.

"Nothing, Mam. Davin's just excited about getting to church this morning." Keeva offered her mother a sweet smile.

Eira narrowed her gaze and pinned Keeva a suspicious glare, then noticed the scarf fluttering on the fence post behind them. "Why is your scarf on Mr. Lubbock's fence? What tomfoolery is afoot?"

"Well, Mam, I simply—"

Before she could offer an explanation, Davin cut in. "She told Oliver and Matthew the one to claim her scarf on the way to church could sit by her today."

"She what?" Eira asked in a loud voice that drew the gazes of fellow travelers heading for the church. Lowering her voice, she glowered at Keeva, disapproval practically radiating from her entire being. "Explain, daughter."

Keeva scrambled for a way to convey the details of the challenge she'd issued to Oliver James and Matthew Baumann yesterday at Mariah

Bainbridge's skating party that would make it sound as harmless as she'd intended it to be. Both boys had made it clear they wanted to court her, and she hadn't yet decided which one she liked better. In the meantime, it had been grand fun to see them battle each other for her affection.

"Yesterday, at Mariah's party, this saucy imp challenged Ollie and Matthew to see who would earn the right to sit beside her during this morning's church service, as if she was a queen bestowing some grand honor." Davin blurted before Keeva could clap a hand over his mouth to silence him. He tossed a teasing grin her way. "For reasons no one will ever know, both of them seem to be daffy over Keeva. I keep telling Ollie he could do much better, like Mariah, for instance, but he seems quite taken with this one."

When Davin reached out to tug on a tendril of hair Keeva had positioned just so by her ear, she slapped his hand, earning an icy scowl from her mother.

"Maureen Keeva Holt! How could you do such a thing?" her mother asked with a dark scowl. "You know Oliver and Matthew get along like two wild cats with their tails knotted together. You might as well have poured kerosene on a blazing fire."

Her mother was only partially correct. Oliver and Matthew had been friends since Matthew's family had moved to town three years ago. The two boys had developed a competitive streak with one another that was wider than the river and three times as deep, causing them to constantly be at odds over one thing or another, but it was mostly all in good nature. Their latest competition had been over Keeva.

"Oh, it's fine, Mam. I just—"

"Sometimes, Keeva, it would behoove you to listen more than you speak." Her father looked back at her, and Keeva snapped her mouth shut. Not often did Hiram Holt speak his mind, but when he did, every member of their family listened.

Eira gave Keeva one more censorious glare before she spun around on the seat, whispered something to Hiram, then shook her head, as though she couldn't believe Keeva was her child.

Keeva loved both of her parents, but the past year, she felt as though she and her mother spent most of their time ramming their heads and tempers together in a most unpleasant manner. Nothing Keeva did seemed to please her mother. She was sure Eira was constantly watching her, waiting to find some miniscule thing to criticize.

Like challenging two dashing young men to claim a seat beside her for the church service this morning.

The truth was, Keeva hadn't told Oliver and Matthew how to compete. She'd merely stated the fellow who arrived at church with her scarf could sit beside her during the service.

Despite the cold and snow, the church yard was full of sleighs and wagons when they arrived. Families hurried inside out of the frosty temperatures, but Keeva lingered a moment, pretending to search for a lost glove.

"Stop dawdling," Davin chided, pulling the supposedly lost glove from her coat pocket.

She felt like smacking him across the back of his head with it but instead quietly pulled it on.

Hiram got out and reached up, settling his hands on Eira's waist, then lifted her down to the ground. Davin stepped out of the sleigh and turned to give Keeva a hand when the sounds of thundering hoofbeats carried in the still winter air. Although it was still snowing, the flakes were light, falling gently as they gave the earth a fresh coating of white, like the fine sugar her mother used to top her decadent apple cake.

Keeva turned in the sleigh and watched as Oliver and Matthew raced each other down the hill. Both young men were tossing taunts to each other and laughing uproariously as they charged along the road, intent on claiming Keeva's scarf.

People who hadn't yet gone into the church stopped to watch the two mischievous young men.

"Those foolish idiots are going to break their necks," Eira said, then grabbed onto Hiram's arm. "Can't you put a stop to it, Hiram?"

"Not at the moment, love. Not until those two make it down the hill." Hiram shook his head and settled a protective arm around his wife, then gave Keeva a look thick with condemnation. "We will be having a conversation this afternoon, daughter."

Keeva dreaded what her father might say but shoved it from her mind. She turned her attention back to her two suitors. They were handsome, charming, funny, and sweet. Outwardly, they were matched in height and width, but they looked nothing alike. Matthew's hair was as pale as whipped butter, while Oliver's shimmered as black as a raven's wing.

Yet, they both had captured Keeva's interest. She'd been unable to choose one over the other, caring for them differently, but equally. The girls at school had been quite jealous of her beaux, but she didn't care. All that mattered was that they adored her and she felt great affection toward them.

When they weren't fighting or jostling to gain her attention, she had a marvelous time with Oliver and Matthew.

Like today.

Excitement coursed through her as she watched the two energetic, athletic young men race their horses down the hill. A few girls hurried closer to the fence around the church yard to watch. Davin climbed back into the sleigh so he could get a better view of the race.

Oliver pulled ahead on his big black horse, then Matthew edged past him on his speckled roan. Back and forth they went while everyone watched, waiting to see who would win.

Suddenly, Keeva wished she'd heeded Davin's warnings yesterday that she was causing trouble. While she didn't mind being the center of Oliver and Matthew's attention, she had no desire for half the church congregation to discover that the reason the two young men rode so recklessly down the hill was because of her.

"I told you," Davin said under his breath as he leaned near her ear, as though he could read her thoughts.

Keeva might have swatted at him and batted his words away, but at that precise moment, Oliver's horse hit a patch of ice.

As though she witnessed it in slow-moving motion, Keeva saw the horse lose its battle to find his footing. One minute the animal was upright, the next it had flipped over on top of Oliver.

"Ollie! No!" Keeva yelled, but her voice was lost in the numerous screams piercing the air.

Matthew drew his horse to a stop, hopped off, and ran over to Oliver. He fell to his knees beside the prone figure of his friend.

The horse lunged to its feet, but before it could run off, Davin jumped out of the sleigh and dashed to catch the reins.

Oliver's head rested at an unnatural angle, his body crumpled and still. Too still. When Matthew released an unearthly, desperate howl of despair, Keeva knew the worst had happened, and it was all her fault.

"No, Ollie. No," she whispered. Everything around her blurred, then faded into darkness.

Chapter Two

"Please, darling girl. Come outside with me. The sun is shining like a glorious golden orb in the sky." Eira stroked Keeva's limp hand as it rested on her lap.

Listless and despondent, Keeva had barely left the house in the two months since Oliver had died. Every time she closed her eyes, she could see the horse flipping over on him, snapping his neck.

According to Davin, Matthew blamed himself, but he was the only one. Keeva felt as though the entire community blamed her. She knew Oliver's parents did. Even after she'd gone to them, pleading and begging for their forgiveness, Oliver's mother had called her Jezebel, and his father had said she was no longer welcome in their home.

The few times she'd ventured out, people stared and pointed, whispering as she walked by. It seemed everyone knew of the challenge she'd given to Oliver and Matthew. Knew that if she hadn't been so haughty and prideful, a fine young man would still be alive.

How could she expect anyone else to forgive her when she refused to forgive herself?

Keeva detested the egotistical girl she'd become. The past two months of her self-inflicted isolation at home had given her far too many hours of introspection. She never again wanted to be the careless, coy person who had caused Oliver's death. In spite of her family's reassurance it wasn't her fault, Keeva couldn't let go of the notion that it was. If she'd never pitted two friends against each other, Oliver would be alive and well, riding his horse around town and joking with Davin and Matthew instead of buried in the cemetery by the church.

"Keeva. You can't spend the rest of your life hiding in this house," Eira said, rising from the window seat, where the two of them had been seated. With an exasperated huff, she pulled Keeva to her feet. "Just because Oliver died doesn't mean you can stop living. You have to go on, Keeva."

"I know, Mam, but it's so hard. I just ... it's just so ..." Keeva sighed. "I don't know what to do."

"I know, baby. I know." Her mother engulfed her in a tight embrace, kissed both of her cheeks, then tugged her outside.

The sun was bright in the early spring sky. Keeva tipped her head back and savored the warmth of it on her face. Other than seeing to her daily chores, she had hardly been outside in weeks. She drew in a deep breath of air tinged with the loamy hint of the earth renewing after the cold winter days. It wouldn't be long before the grass turned green, the trees began to bud, and flowers bloomed.

Keeva couldn't imagine spending all summer hiding in the house, but she was unable to envision spending her days outdoors as she had in the past. Not when someone might happen along to remind her of the devastation she'd caused to the James family and the whole community through her foolishness.

The pastor at their church had tried to talk to her numerous times, but Keeva wasn't of a mind to listen. Not now. Maybe never. Not when she felt so ashamed of her actions.

Her father had told her it was acceptable to make mistakes if you learned from them. Keeva had certainly learned a lesson from what she'd done to Oliver and Matthew. She would never again act like such a flirtatious ninny. In fact, she'd decided she'd remain single the rest of her days as penance for the tragedy she'd caused.

"Isn't it lovely out?" Her mother gave her an indulgent smile. "Come on, Keeva. Some of the flowers are starting to push their way up through the soil, just reaching out to welcome springtime."

Keeva smiled in spite of herself. Eira Holt may be mother to seven children, and she may dote on her ten grandchildren, but she was often full of fancy and fairy dust, as Hiram liked to say.

After spending an hour outside, Keeva returned to the kitchen with her mother to begin supper preparations. As she peeled potatoes, she thought about how good it had felt to be outside again. Perhaps she could spend a little more time outside each day, but she wouldn't dare go into town. Would she spend the rest of her life cowering on the farm, hoping eventually the people in town would forget her transgressions?

By pure accident, she'd caught tidbits of conversations between her parents, expressing their concerns for her. She didn't want to be a burden to them, but she had no idea what she could do.

A few days later, the answer presented itself in the form of a birthday gift from her family.

Keeva had all but forgotten her birthday although months ago she'd been so looking forward to turning eighteen.

Naively, she'd thought simply changing her age would make her all grown up. She'd since learned that growing up wasn't determined by the calendar, but by life experiences and how one faced them.

She felt old beyond her years as her family gathered to share birthday wishes with her and eat the decadent chocolate cake her mother had baked. Once the dishes were cleared away, an assortment of gifts appeared on the dining table.

Her father cleared his throat and glanced at Eira. She moved behind Keeva's chair, standing with her hands on her shoulders as Hiram took an envelope from the pocket of his overalls and handed it to Keeva.

"In light of current circumstances, we thought this might be the best gift we could give you this year, daughter."

Keeva took the envelope from him, opened the flap, and pulled out a train ticket to Holiday, Oregon, where her favorite brother, Evan, lived with his wife. When he had married Henley last year, Keeva and Davin had accompanied their parents to the ceremony. Keeva had loved the little town in the mountains of Eastern Oregon. Henley and Evan both had told her she was welcome to visit whenever she liked.

For the first time since Oliver's death, Keeva felt a flicker of hope begin to burn in her heart. No one in Holiday would know what had happened. No one there would judge her. No one would give her angry or pitying stares. There, she could just be Doctor Evan Holt's sister.

She glanced at her father, then looked over her shoulder at her mother. Eira nodded her head and smiled in understanding. Keeva leaped out of her seat and hugged first her mother, then her father.

"Thank you so much, Mam and Dad. This is more than a gift. It's hope."

Her mother dabbed at her tears, and her father cleared his throat a second time as he gave her another hug, lifting her off her feet before he set her down and pointed to the other gifts on the table.

"You'd better open the rest," he said, his voice raspy with emotion.

It seemed her siblings had been aware of her parents' plans to send her on a trip. Her two oldest brothers and their wives had gone together to purchase Keeva a lovely traveling satchel. Her sister Fianna gifted her with a set of stationery and a pen set. Davin gave her a new hat that matched a beautiful gown her oldest sister, a seamstress, had created for her.

"I feel so spoiled and loved," Keeva said, unable to hold back her tears. "Thank you all for this. I won't let this gift be a waste. It will truly be a new beginning for me."

"We'll miss you so, darling girl," her mother said, hugging her again. "But you need to see possibilities when you look out your window instead of painful memories."

"Thank you, Mam and Dad. Thank you all for these wonderful gifts, and for loving me when I needed it most."

Even Davin's eyes welled with unshed tears as Keeva hugged and thanked each of them again.

Although her parents suggested waiting until May to make the trip, Keeva felt an urgency to leave behind the sadness of her past and step into what she hoped would become a much brighter future.

Three days later, after a flurry of packing, her whole family gathered again at the train depot to bid her farewell. At her request, no one had informed Evan or Henley of her plans to travel to Holiday. They'd all agreed it would be grand for her to surprise them.

"Are you sure you don't want me to come along?" Davin asked for the tenth time since Keeva had announced her intentions to leave right away. "I'm not so sure you'll be safe traveling alone."

"I'll be fine, Davin, but thank you for your concern." She kissed her brother's cheek, then hugged her father and mother one last time before she accepted the porter's hand and climbed up the steps to the train car. "I love you all!" She blew them a kiss, then stepped inside the car.

The basket she carried was filled with food that would keep on her trip. Her satchel was packed with essentials she might need for the journey, as well as a change of clothes. Tucked into an old sock her mother had stitched into the bag's lining was every penny Keeva had saved. A hundred dollars had seemed like a fortune before, but now it seemed very little with which to begin a new life.

Her father had tucked a twenty-dollar gold piece into her hand as they'd left the house that morning.

"Just in case you need it on your way to Holiday," he'd said, making her weepy once again.

Keeva felt as though her emotions had been bouncing between elation and despair since the evening of her birthday. She was thrilled to go to Holiday and spend time with Evan, but she felt anguished by the fact that she was leaving behind her family in Altoona and had no idea when she'd see them again.

The past two months, she and her mother had shared a closeness they'd never known. Keeva hated to leave now, uncertain if things between them would change with so many miles separating them.

Before Oliver had died, Keeva had been so confident and self-sure, she'd all but pushed her mother away. It had been her behavior that had caused the rift between them, not anything her mother had done.

The past two months had brought blessings intertwined with the burdens. If nothing else, the experiences she'd endured had helped her reconcile with her mother.

"Make sure you let us know you made it there in one piece," her father called as Keeva opened the window and looked outside.

"I will. I promise! Goodbye! I love you all!" She waved a gloved hand out the window, then closed it and took her seat as the train began rolling forward. Keeva settled her satchel between her leg and the wall of the train car, then slid the basket of food beneath the seat.

Settled and ready for adventure, she placed her hands on her lap and fixed her gaze out the window, giddy to see something beyond her family's farm.

Chapter Three

"Holiday, folks! Welcome to Holiday!" the conductor called as he walked through the train car several days later. The train, pulled by an engine with the word *Hope* painted across the side of it, rolled smoothly into the station.

Keeva nearly bounced on her seat as she looked out the window at the lush green of the mountains. After quickly gathering her satchel and the empty food basket, she was the third person to exit the car.

With a spring in her step that had been absent since January, she walked across the platform and inhaled a deep breath of the pine-scented air. It smelled so fresh and green and invigorating.

For the trip, Keeva had dressed in a somber gray suit one of her sisters-in-law had outgrown and a black fedora that was adorned with only one ribbon tied into a conservative bow. During the days of travel, she'd done her best to curtail her natural inclination to be friendly and engaging. She quietly watched out the window or used the pencil and writing tablet she'd brought along to write down her thoughts of the journey. She would make a copy of her notes and send it to her family with her first letter home.

Now that she was in Holiday, the tight bands that had been squeezing the life from her suddenly released, and she felt she could once again breathe.

The desire to yank off her hat and tug her hair free from the pins that confined it in a severe knot at the back of her head was strong, but she resisted.

Instead, she stepped into the depot and waited in line to speak to the stationmaster.

"Good afternoon, sir," she said, smiling politely at him.

"Howdy, miss. What can I do for you?" he asked while stamping a paper and setting it aside, not bothering to look up at her.

"I'm hopeful I might leave my trunks in your care until I can have my brother retrieve them. It shouldn't be long. I just need to let him know they are here," she said, watching as the man stamped two more pages, scribbled something on one of them, and added them to the stack to his right.

"And who might your brother be?" he asked, glanced up at her, then gave her a second, more intent look. "You're Doc's sister, aren't you?"

Keeva grinned. "I am Evan's sister. I believe we met when I came for his wedding last year."

"That's right. That's right," he said, setting down the stamp and pencil in his hands. "Welcome back to Holiday, Miss Holt. Don't worry about your trunks. I'll have one of the lads run them over to Doc's place. Just point out where they are," he said, stepping around the counter and following Keeva to the door.

"Those three right there," she said, pointing to her small stack sitting amongst a pile of other trunks.

The stationmaster whistled, and a gangly boy who looked to be twelve or thirteen set a trunk into a wagon that was backed up to the platform, then raced over.

"Yes, sir?" the boy asked politely.

The stationmaster pointed to Keeva's trunks. "Tommy. Would you load those three trunks and take them to Doc's place?"

"Sure, Mr. Masters." Tommy tipped his cap to Keeva, then hastened to see to her trunks.

Keeva smiled at the stationmaster. "Thank you, Mr. Masters. I'm grateful for your assistance."

"Of course. Anything for Doc and his family. Have a nice visit, Miss Holt."

She nodded at the man. "I intend to. Thank you."

She walked down the platform steps and made her way out to the street. It wasn't far to Evan's home, at least if she correctly recalled the way from her last visit. She walked past the express office and a building that had *Fire Department* painted on the window, then turned and crossed the street.

Evan's house and office looked just as she recalled. The fence surrounding his property shone white against the background of green grass and the blue sky dotted with fluffy clouds. She pictured how it would look when the flowers began to bloom. Two rockers sat on the front porch, and a sign on the corner post pointed to the door where patients entered her brother's medical practice.

Keeva spied Evan's cat, Tuesday, lazing in a patch of sunshine on the far end of the porch. Quietly, she walked up the porch steps, set her basket and satchel on one of the rocking chairs, then went over to the cat, letting him sniff her fingers after she removed her gloves. He blinked at her and started to purr. Keeva gave him several good scratches beneath his chin and around his ears before she pulled on her gloves, picked up her things, and walked around the side of the house to the door to Evan's practice.

She stepped inside and heard the bell over the door jingle as her gaze took in a miner sitting in a chair with a bloody rag wrapped around his arm, a mother with a screaming toddler squirming on her lap, and an old man holding a cloth to one of his back teeth. The scent of cloves mingled with the smell of medicine and disinfectant.

Keeva took a shallow breath and shifted her gaze to the doorway of the hall as footsteps neared.

"Good afternoon. Doctor Holt will be with you as soon as he can. How may we help you today?" a beautiful blonde woman with an angelic face asked as she took a seat at the desk and dipped a pen in the inkwell without looking up to see who had entered.

"Let's begin with a welcoming hug, Henley," Keeva said, grinning at her sister-in-law.

Her smile widened as she watched Henley glance up at her in surprise, then she hopped up from the chair, skirted the desk, and engulfed Keeva in a hug.

"Oh, my gracious!" Henley pulled back with a wide smile, then hugged her again. "Is it really you, Keeva? What on earth are you doing in Holiday? If you sent word you were coming, we didn't receive it."

"I wanted to surprise you." Keeva took a step back and lifted her hands to her sides. "Surprise!"

Henley laughed. "Evan will be so pleased to see you. He's rather occupied at the moment. Why don't you go on in the house and make yourself at home? He'll be in just as soon as he can."

Keeva nodded in understanding. "I'll leave my things there. Mr. Masters is having someone bring over my trunks. While I wait for their delivery, I'll dash over to the telegraph office and send a note to let Mam and Dad know I've arrived safe and sound."

"You do that. I'll keep an eye out for Tommy. Or was it Jimmy bringing your trunks?"

"Tommy, and thank you, Henley." Keeva walked with her down the hallway past Evan's examination rooms and office and opened the door into the house he shared with Henley. It was small. Only one bedroom, which Keeva had forgotten. Would they even have room for her trunks? She could sleep on their couch or the floor, at least until she figured out what to do with herself.

She had no intention of being a burden to her brother, especially since he and Henley hadn't even

DREAMS WITH FAITH

been married a year. In fact, it was about this time last year that they'd met on the train carrying them to Holiday. Evan had just been home for Fianna's wedding, and Henley had been traveling as a mail-order bride. Her would-be groom had struck gold and left town before she'd arrived.

Anyone with eyes in their head could see how much Henley and Evan loved each other, so it seemed everything worked out just as it was supposed to. God's plans were a mystery, and sometimes Keeva needed a reminder about that truth.

Keeva set her satchel on a chair and the basket on the counter in the kitchen, then hurried to the telegraph office, where she sent her parents a brief message. She knew Henley wasn't much of a cook although she was learning, and Evan would appreciate a good meal. With a menu in mind, Keeva headed to the mercantile and purchased what she'd need to make supper.

She was waiting on the corner for a lumber wagon to pass when she glanced across the street at the church.

The pastor who had performed Henley and Evan's wedding ceremony was nothing like she had expected. In fact, John Ryan was young and handsome, and had lingered in Keeva's thoughts long after they'd returned home from Holiday last year.

As she crossed the street and headed toward Evan's home, she wondered if he would remember her.

Chapter Four

John Ryan crossed out the line he'd just written. He couldn't find the right wording to begin his Sunday sermon and had rewritten the opening paragraph so many times his thoughts were completely jumbled.

Annoyed with himself, he wadded the piece of paper into a ball and lobbed it into the wire trash basket by his desk.

With a frustrated sigh, he stood and walked over to the window, pushing aside the curtain to look outside. It was a beautiful spring day in Holiday.

Feeling called to travel out West, he'd left his home in Maine six years ago. At the time, he'd never expected to end up in the growing mountain town in Eastern Oregon. In fact, when he'd first arrived, Holiday had barely been more than a rough mining camp. However, it was rapidly changing, especially as more families moved into the area and more businesses opened.

Originally, John figured he'd be in Holiday a year or two, then move on, but he hadn't felt a nudge to leave. In truth, he loved living in the small town. The air was crisp and fresh and clean. The mountains around them were incredible. He loved the community, and especially those who attended the church he pastored. Granted, it was the only church in Holiday, but he was pleased to see how the congregation had steadily grown along with the population of the town.

It would only be a matter of time before more churches popped up, but for now, he did his best to nourish the souls of those who faithfully attended his services.

John pushed open the window, closed his eyes, and drank in the refreshing breeze. He drew a second cleansing breath, then opened his eyes. His gaze widened, and he leaned out the window, convinced he was seeing things. Across the street, waiting for a wagon to pass, was a woman who bore a striking resemblance to Keeva Holt, Doctor Evan Holt's younger sister.

When Evan's parents and two of his siblings had traveled to Holiday last year for his wedding, John had found himself fascinated with Keeva. She possessed a personality as vibrant as her bright red curly hair. The girl was far too young for him, not to mention she seemed half-wild and utterly unpredictable.

Still, she was a beauty, and her smile made it seem like sunbeams gleamed from it. The few times he'd interacted directly with her, she'd been full of laughter and fun.

While that might be fine for some men, John had it settled in his mind what would be expected of a pastor's wife. She should be meek, soft-spoken, gentle, quiet, and kind. She wouldn't call attention to herself or stand out in a crowd. The perfect wife for him would be one who wanted to humbly dedicate her life to serving God and others. Not some free-spirited lass with a head full of fiery curls.

John leaned farther out the window, watching as the woman crossed the street. Even her steps seemed energetic and full of life as she fairly bounced to the other side of the street. Keeva, if it was her, lacked the subdued tread of a refined female.

About to fall out the window head-first as he ogled the woman walking in the direction of the doctor's office, John pulled himself back in so abruptly, he smacked his head on the window in the process.

Already irritated, he felt fury bubbling in his chest as he rubbed the back of his head with one hand and curled the other into a fist. The urge to punch something was nearly overwhelming, preferably himself for thinking the thoughts he'd entertained about Miss Keeva Holt.

Even her name was unusual and stood out.

Why couldn't she be a Rebecca, or a Martha, or even an Elizabeth? Why couldn't her hair be a plain hue of brown? Or her eyes a dull shade of gray instead of verdant green like emeralds reflecting summer sunlight?

John sighed. Who was he to think the Creator had made a mistake with the girl?

Keeva wasn't plain because God hadn't made her to be subdued, quiet, or meek. She was full of life and exuberance. From the freckles sprinkling her nose to the way she fairly danced on her toes, Keeva was … Keeva.

Admittedly, John had thought of her many times since her visit to Holiday the previous summer. He'd recalled the way her hair had looked with the sun setting it aflame. How her lips had appeared so rosy and lush. How her nose wrinkled ever so slightly when she laughed, which was often.

"Enough!" he shouted, then hoped no one passing by outside heard him. "Pull yourself together, man," he chastised in a much quieter tone. John bowed his head and prayed for forgiveness for entertaining wayward thoughts in the first place as well as his rising temper.

He felt marginally better when he finished his prayer.

Keeva was a temptation he simply needed to resist. If the woman he'd just seen was in fact Keeva, he'd avoid her as much as possible until she returned to Pennsylvania.

In the meantime, John would work harder at finding a suitable wife. He was twenty-six now, and it was time for him to wed. To find a true helpmate who would be a partner in his ministry, like his grandmother had always been to his grandfather.

John had grown up attending the church his grandfather had pastored. Grandpa Otis had been the reason John had wanted to go into the ministry. Seeing the faithful way his grandparents had lived and the caring way they had treated others had inspired him to want to serve God.

His parents hadn't been thrilled with his calling. John's father was a farmer and expected all six of his sons to help on the place. John's three older brothers had been able to purchase nearby ground and expand the family farming operations. His two younger brothers worked alongside their father. Four of his brothers had already wed, and three had started families of their own.

John missed his nieces and nephews and joking with his brothers, but he didn't particularly miss the long, tiring hours of working on the farm. He didn't miss rising long before the sun to milk cows and feed animals, or toiling beneath the scorching sun to plant, tend, and harvest their crops.

Even if he hadn't minded the hard work, he had never felt the urge to farm. He'd always been drawn to the Bible and sharing God's word with others.

Once, when he was seven, he'd stood on the bench outside the mercantile while his mother shopped, held his little Bible in his hand, and orated about the gift of salvation. Several people had stopped to listen, no doubt amused at the way he so perfectly mimicked his grandfather.

His mother had not been amused, his father had been embarrassed, and John had never again used the bench at the mercantile as his pulpit. But even after his father had paddled his backside, it hadn't dimmed his yearning to share God's truth with others. So, he'd gone against his parents' wishes and become a minister anyway.

"It's a good thing," he said to himself as he plopped back down at his desk and once again picked up his pencil. "If I weren't focused on my work, I'd let someone like Keeva Holt turn my head."

Of course, that would never, ever do.

It took John two and a half hours to finally complete a sermon he felt carried a message that would feed his flock. He left it on his desk to read over tomorrow. He liked to write his sermons on Friday afternoons so he had time to think about the message, make changes that appealed to him, and then practice delivering his oration a few times before Sunday morning arrived.

Eager to stretch his muscles, John shrugged into a light jacket, even though it was plenty warm outside without one. He didn't feel properly attired without his shirtsleeves covered and a hat on his head. He tugged on his hat, opened the door, and stepped out into the spring sunshine.

With no particular direction in mind, he wandered along Main Street. He walked all the way out to R.C. Milton's blacksmith shop and livery. He waved at the man, then turned along Milton Road and walked down to the depot and engine house, then changed direction and headed back toward the church.

It wasn't out of the ordinary that his steps carried him past Evan and Henley Holt's home. If Keeva was visiting, John briefly wondered where she would stay. The doctor's house was small, with his clinic taking up a good portion of the space. To John's knowledge, there was only one bedroom. Evan did have a recovery room for patients who required overnight stays. Maybe she would sleep there. Perhaps Keeva would take a room at the hotel. If she did, Edith Piedmont would ensure she had a comfortable stay.

The fact that he was mulling over Keeva's sleeping arrangements only served to agitate him. He must stop considering the woman. Girl, really. She was only eighteen. He recalled her mentioning her birthday was at the end of March. Since it was the second of April, she was technically a year older than the last time he'd seen her. He wondered if she was wiser. More mature. More settled in life.

Or if she would still be as flighty as a fidgety fairy.

"Stop thinking about her," he grumbled under his breath and broke into a trot, determined to head home before someone caught him talking to himself and arrived at the conclusion that he was on the verge of losing his mind.

At the moment, John might have agreed with them. He felt like he was losing it—over Keeva Holt.

Chapter Five

"Good morning," John said, standing at the door and greeting members of the congregation as they arrived. He nodded politely to the Coleman family. Grant Coleman had been one of the first people to arrive in the area, building up Elk Creek Ranch from nothing.

His son Jace walked in behind him, his hand at the waist of his lovely wife, Cora Lee. When Cora Lee had first arrived in town, John had seriously contemplated courting the woman. She fit the mold he had in his mind of what a pastor's wife should be. Cora Lee was fair of face, which didn't matter, but it wasn't exactly a detriment. In fact, she was quite beautiful, but more than that, she was kind, gentle, giving, generous, and selfless. She was also the most incredible cook he'd ever met. Thoughts of the last meal he'd eaten out at the ranch made his mouth water.

"If you don't already have plans for lunch, Pastor Ryan, will you join us today?" Jace asked as he and Cora Lee paused to greet him.

"I'd enjoy that. Thank you." John smiled at them with warmth and gratitude. He tried not to accept their frequent invitations. It wasn't that he didn't want to eat with them. He would have gladly pulled up a chair at their table every Sunday. But invitations to Sunday lunches gave him an opportunity to visit members of the congregation and get to know them better, so he tried to accept an invite from someone different every week. From dining at the tables of various homes in Holiday and surrounding farms and ranches, he knew the best and worst cooks in the area.

Thank goodness Jace had invited him before Mrs. Lymon had a chance. The widow hadn't been subtle in her pursuit of him, forcing him to get quite good at evasive measures. The woman's husband had died in a mining accident more than a year ago, leaving her with no income. She'd started doing laundry and taking in mending, but John had no doubt it was hard for her to manage on the small income she made. Regardless of how much he pitied her situation, he had no interest in marrying Mrs. Lymon. The woman was shaped like a barrel, had a tendency to gossip, and was mother to three of the unruliest children John had ever encountered.

Before Mrs. Lymon waddled up the steps, John backed away from the door and made his way to the front of the church. He focused on the notes he'd left on the pulpit, rehearsing his sermon in his mind one more time as the last members of the congregation filed in.

He glanced up and saw Evan and Henley Holt take a seat in their usual pew. A woman who was standing with her back to John turned and sat beside Henley. When she looked up, their gazes collided. John felt as though a lightning bolt struck him as he recognized Keeva.

His imagination hadn't just conjured her. She really was in Holiday. In his church, shyly smiling at him from her seat with her brother and his wife.

"Focus, focus, focus," John chanted under his breath. He cleared his throat, straightened his posture, and forced a smile. "Good morning, friends. Welcome to Holiday Community Church. Let's begin this morning's service by singing hymn twenty-one. 'Abide With Me.' Thank you, Mrs. Milton, for leading the singing this morning. Hymn twenty-one."

John sang the words by memory. At the moment, he was incapable of paying attention to the words or focusing on the hymnbook. His thoughts tumbled over and around each other wondering what brought Keeva to Holiday, and why Evan hadn't mentioned her impending arrival. Was she in town for a short visit? A long stay? Indefinitely?

Good lands!

What if the woman had decided to move to Holiday?

John stumbled over the words to a hymn he'd sung all his life as his musings about Keeva nearly sent him into a fit of panic. By sheer determination, he slammed the door to his ponderings and forced his attention back to the morning service.

He asked Grant Coleman to deliver the opening prayer, then gave an abbreviated version of his sermon while the collar around his throat grew tighter and tighter with each glance that landed on Keeva's enchanting face. After singing one more hymn, John offered the closing prayer and somehow managed to read through the announcements he'd written out.

"Thank you all for being here this morning. May your week ahead be blessed and joyous." John nodded to his congregation, then stepped down from the pulpit and made his way to the back door, which he pushed open. He gulped in a few breaths of fresh air before turning to greet people as they filed out of the church.

He couldn't help but cast a few glances toward the Holt family, watching as Cora Lee and Anne Milton gave Keeva welcoming hugs. Keeva quickly latched onto Anne's baby boy. Distracted by the way she cuddled the little one, he didn't realize Grant Coleman was waiting to shake his hand until the man cleared his throat.

John shook Grant's hand.

The rancher grinned at him. "I enjoyed the sermon this morning, John. Brief and to the point. You wouldn't happen to have something on your mind, would you?"

Mortified to have been caught gawking at Keeva, John shook his head. "Nothing particular, Grant. Thank you for being here this morning. I am looking forward to sharing lunch with you today."

"Good. Jace said you were coming. We'll see you at the ranch." Grant tipped his head, settled his hat on it, and strode out the door.

John turned slightly so Keeva was out of his line of sight and continued shaking hands. He accepted a hearty clasp from his best friend, Marshal Dillon Durant. Dillon's beautiful bride, Zara, beamed as she walked beside him. It appeared marriage quite suited his friend.

Mrs. Lymon shoved her way between Dillon and Zara and grabbed onto John's hand, shaking it so hard he felt like his shoulder might pop out of joint. "Will you join us for lunch, Pastor Ryan?" she asked with a hopeful look on her face.

"I'm sorry, Mrs. Lymon, I've already made plans, but I do appreciate your thinking of me. Perhaps another time."

"Next Sunday it is!"

"Oh, he won't be able to next Sunday," Zara said, smiling sweetly as she took a step closer to John. "He's promised to join us for lunch. The Sunday after that I believe is already planned as well."

"Well, I'll catch you one of these days, Pastor." Mrs. Lymon gave him a miffed look, then marched out the door. He watched her gather her ornery boys and head away from the church yard on foot.

John turned to Zara with a grateful smile and lowered his voice so only she and Dillon could hear. "Thank you for saving me from what will surely be a most unpleasant experience. You don't really have to invite me to lunch next week."

"But we do. We actually meant to anyway," Zara hurried to assure him, and Dillon nodded in agreement. "Nan mentioned wanting you to come out soon. If she weren't still down with a case of the sniffles, she would have been here to invite you herself."

Nan Nichols was an elderly widow who had taken Dillon under her wing. His friend doted on the older woman, and Nan treated Dillon and Zara like beloved grandchildren. John was thankful they all had each other.

In fact, he'd never seen Dillon as happy as he'd been since meeting Zara back in August when she'd arrived to teach school. Holiday had been having a terrible time keeping teachers. Up until Zara, every teacher they'd employed had left to go mine, sure they'd find gold.

Zara had been a blessing to the students, their parents, and the community, but especially to Dillon. After growing up in an orphanage and becoming hardened by work in Texas as a lawman, Dillon had made his way out west. He hadn't been planning to take a wife, but after he met Zara, it was quite clear he'd quickly lost his heart to the lovely woman with an equally lovely heart.

John was so pleased for his friend, and for Zara, to have found happiness and love with one another.

However, he was sure he'd never find it if he continued letting women like Keeva Holt turn his head. Actually, Keeva was the only one who had turned his head, and John didn't like it. Not one bit.

He'd have to spend some time in prayer, seeking guidance where she was concerned.

For now, though, he looked forward to a delicious meal with the Coleman family, and an afternoon of laughter. Nearly every Sunday found the Milton family gathered around the table at Elk Creek Ranch. Jace and R.C. were always primed for joking and teasing one another, which provided entertainment for everyone.

Evan and Henley each shook his hand and stepped outside. Keeva was the last to leave, still holding the Miltons' baby.

"Well, Miss Holt. What a surprise to see you in Holiday this morning. Are you visiting your brother?"

"For a while," she said cryptically.

He was thankful the baby kept both of her hands occupied. He recalled feeling something zap his fingers and trail up his arm when they'd shaken hands last summer. He hadn't liked that unsettling feeling then, and was sure he wouldn't enjoy it now.

Before he could say anything in response, she offered him a polite nod and hurried out the door. When she cast him a glance over her shoulder, John's gaze once again collided with hers. Something magnetic pulled at him, and he took a step toward her before he realized he was about to chase after her. That would not do. Not at all.

Quickly shutting the door to the church, he sagged against it and released a pent-up breath.

Normally, he set the church to rights following the service, but for once, it could wait. He went into the church office he rarely used and out the side door, which brought him close to the gate that let him through the fence into his home's side yard.

After hurrying inside his house, John changed out of his best suit into a pair of denims and a plaid cotton shirt and grabbed a light jacket and a hat that had seen better days. Hastily shoving his feet into a pair of worn boots, he hurried outside and jogged through town to the livery. He caught R.C. and Anne just as they were about to leave.

"Mind if I catch a ride with you?" he asked.

R.C. grinned. "Not a bit. Should we assume you are heading to Elk Creek Ranch for lunch?"

"You may assume that." John smiled and slid onto the back seat of the buggy. "I appreciate the ride. If I hadn't caught you, I would have had to saddle Esau myself."

Anne glanced over her shoulder at him. "I still can't fathom why you named that beautiful horse Esau. He's not overly hairy."

John shrugged. "Just seemed like a good name for him. I don't think he cares."

"Likely not," Anne said, adjusting the baby in her arms. The way Keeva had been clinging to him, he was almost surprised the girl had returned Charles to his mother.

Keeva had been even prettier than he'd remembered. Her hair was still just as fiery red, her eyes a verdant field of green, but something was different about her. She seemed more … mature, perhaps. More something, anyway.

More beautiful, for certain. More stunning. More intriguing. More fascinating. More …

John pulled his thoughts up short and shoved them to the far corners of his mind. He leaned forward slightly, glancing over Anne's shoulder at the baby, who looked so much like his father.

"So, has little Charles been sleeping through the night, or is he still keeping you both awake at all hours?" John mentally congratulated himself on finding a topic that was sure to keep R.C. and Anne talking for at least part of the ride out to the ranch.

After they exhausted the conversation about Charles' sleeping and eating habits, R.C. inquired about John's family back in Maine. He'd received a letter earlier in the week from his brother Mark's wife. Lisbeth had been friends with John all through their school years and had continued their friendship after she'd wed Mark. She was the one who wrote newsy letters, keeping him updated on the family and their farms. He wrote back, sharing about life in Holiday, how much he enjoyed his congregation, and his friends.

By the time he gave R.C. and Anne a brief update on his siblings and parents, they'd arrived at Elk Creek Ranch. The idyllic setting never failed to give him reason to pause and marvel at the wonders of the Creator.

Pleased and content, he turned from watching horses run across the pasture to see Keeva step out of Evan's buggy. He felt the smile drip right off his face as she tossed her hat on the buggy seat and the sun set the red coils of her hair aflame. The Creator had certainly made a beautiful creation in Keeva Holt.

"Do you mind holding Charles for just a moment, John?" Anne asked, drawing his attention from Keeva back to the moment.

Accustomed to holding his nieces and nephews, John took the little one and made silly faces until he earned a chortle while R.C. helped Anne out of the buggy.

"He likes you, John," R.C. said, grinning as he picked up a basket in one hand but continued holding Anne's hand in the other.

John followed as the two of them led the way into the house.

Grant stood at the door, greeting everyone with warm smiles. "Come in, come in. Welcome! So glad you could join us." The rancher reached for Charles before John had barely stepped inside the large living room. "I'll just take this little fellow off your hands, John."

"You have to share, Pops," Jace warned as he carried a stack of plates to the long dining table. "You can't hog him all afternoon like you usually tend to do."

Grant feigned affront, then kissed the baby's rosy cheek. "Charlie doesn't mind, do you little fella?"

The baby waved his chubby hands and laughed, making everyone smile.

"And his name isn't Charlie," Jace said, scowling at his father.

"Hear that, Charlie?" Grant asked in a mock whisper, leaning close to the baby's ear. "Jace doesn't even know your name."

Jace rolled his eyes as he expelled an exasperated sigh. Anne and Henley helped him set the table, while R.C. set the basket he carried near the couch.

John shoved his hands in his pockets and glanced around only to find Keeva watching him. She dropped her gaze and moved to stand beside Evan. Her brother placed his hand on her shoulder, and the two of them moved into the kitchen to help Cora Lee as she dished up the food.

Once they were all seated, John found himself directly across from Keeva, doing his best not to watch her every move.

"We're honored to have you join us today, John. Would you offer a word of thanks for us?" Grant asked.

John nodded, then bowed his head and offered a prayer of thanks for their time together and asked a blessing on the food as well as each one gathered around the table.

Before long, plates were filled, and conversation flowed.

"Did you see the article in the newspaper about missionaries flocking to China?" Evan asked John as he passed him a bowl of creamy mashed potatoes. "It mentioned a great need due to growing interest there."

"I did see that article. It's wonderful there are opportunities opening up there." John briefly considered if spreading the message of salvation in a foreign land would rid him of his interest in Keeva.

Somehow, he doubted it, and he truly had no interest in serving anywhere beyond America. He felt like he'd traveled a world away from his family as it was. What would it be like if an entire ocean separated them, instead of just several days of train travel?

When they'd eaten their fill, R.C. leaned back in his chair and grinned as he looked around the table. "A woman stormed up to the front desk in a New York City library. Affronted, she said, 'half of these books aren't worth reading.' A bystander gave her a disparaging look, waved his arm around the vast collection of books, and said, 'then read the other half.'"

John joined the others in laughing. Jace told a few funny stories he'd heard during the week, and Evan relayed the latest entertaining news of going out to Mr. Wagner's place to treat a donkey that had gotten its foot stuck in a jar.

"At least he didn't bring Alwena into the clinic," Evan said with a relieved sigh.

"Who is Alwena?" Keeva asked, entering the conversation.

"The donkey."

More laughter ensued. The conversation turned to people they all knew, events on the horizon, and Keeva's arrival.

"What's this I hear about you changing your name?" Cora Lee asked Keeva with a curious expression.

Keeva's cheeks turned pink. "I decided now that I'm grown up, it's time to move beyond all the things of my childhood. My given name is Maureen

Keeva. I was thinking about going by Maureen. It seems more mature."

"I happen to like your name," Cora Lee said.

"Me too," Henley said, placing an arm around Keeva's shoulders. "I think Keeva is a beautiful name, but if you want to be known as Maureen, that is completely up to you."

Keeva nodded and glanced around the table, as though hoping someone would change the subject.

"How long will you be able to stay?" Anne asked as she took a fussing Charles from Grant and swayed back and forth with him.

"Until Evan and Henley grow tired of me, I suppose." Keeva shrugged, her eyes downcast as she twined her napkin into a rope and wrapped it around and around her fingers.

John wondered why such a simple question made her act so nervously. Not that it was any of his business, but something was stealing Keeva's joy. He couldn't fix whatever it was, but he could certainly pray for her to find peace. In fact, he vowed he would do that very thing each time she popped into his thoughts. It would be a better use of his time than pining after a woman who was completely ill-suited to him, no matter how much he might wish otherwise.

Anne excused herself to one of the bedrooms to nurse Charles, and everyone helped clear the table. Keeva and Cora Lee engaged in a conversation about cooking and exchanged recipes, while the men did the dishes. R.C. went to check on Anne while Henley wiped down the table, then everyone was ready for an afternoon of fun.

"It's so nice today, let's sit outside," Cora Lee suggested, leading the way out to the yard, where there were chairs and benches set around. Once everyone was seated, Henley asked Anne and Jace to sing.

Anne handed Charles to Cora Lee, then moved to stand beside Jace. The two of them began with one of John's favorite hymns. Their delightful harmony was a balm to his soul. He leaned back on a bench and listened to them sing a variety of popular music, ballads, and hymns.

While Jace and Anne sang, he watched Keeva out of the corner of his eye. She sat beside her brother and seemed completely absorbed in the music, when she wasn't making silly faces at baby Charles.

A vision of her holding a little boy with her red hair and his blue eyes nearly made John fall off the bench. What in the world was he thinking?

Clearly, he wasn't. It seemed as if his ability to hold onto a rational thought had fled the moment he'd realized Keeva had returned to Holiday.

Would she really change her name? Not that Maureen wasn't a very nice name, but Keeva was Keeva. It suited her perfectly, even if he had pondered what she'd be like if she had a more common name.

The part of him that was good at reading people concluded Keeva was standing at a crossroads in her life, searching for the best direction to move forward. The only one who could choose her path was Keeva, but he would happily offer guidance if she sought his advice.

Then again, who was he to give anyone advice when he couldn't keep Keeva out of his thoughts for more than five minutes at a time?

"Okay, last song," Jace said, nodding to Anne, who looked tired and thirsty.

They finished their impromptu concert by singing a newer hymn John had only heard a few times, but he hummed along to "God Be with You Till We Meet Again." He thought it was an exceptionally fine choice to end the singing.

"Everyone is probably thirsty and ready for dessert," Cora Lee said, handing Charles to Jace, then hurrying inside. Keeva and Henley hopped up and followed her.

Soon, they were all enjoying glasses of cool lemonade and slices of a rich cake loaded with dried fruits and spices and topped with almonds.

"This cake is a wonder, Cora Lee. I'll have to get the recipe, if you are of a mind to share," Keeva said, after taking her third bite. John knew how many she'd tried since he'd been watching her fork travel from her plate to her rosy lips. Lips he realized he desperately wanted to kiss.

Yanking his thoughts back in line, he focused on his own slice of delicious cake.

"I'll happily share the recipe. It's one that Pops' mother passed down to his sister, and she shared it with me." Cora Lee smiled at her father-in-law. "It's a good thing Mae wrote down your favorite recipes, or you'd have to wait until her next visit to enjoy some of the dishes you like so well."

"I'm glad she wrote them down, too, although you do a fine job keeping marvelous meals on the table, honey." Grant winked at her, then forked a big bite of cake and shoved it in his mouth.

Conversation turned from recipes to heritages. Evan and Keeva were unmistakably Irish with English thrown in from their father's side of the family. Grant Coleman had Scottish ancestors. Anne had been born and raised in England. R.C. had no idea about his ancestry, and Henley didn't know much about hers.

"What about you, John?" Jace asked.

"My ancestors?" John questioned.

Jace nodded. "Where do they come from?"

"To my knowledge, they all came from England at one point or another. My grandmother's family claims to have crossed the ocean on the Mayflower, but no one ever produced any proof."

"Wouldn't that be something?" Henley said, smiling wistfully. "It's quite a thing to imagine, isn't it? Arriving in a new land, forging a new life."

Anne grinned at her. "And what is it you think we've all done?"

Henley laughed. "Exactly that. Left the known to step into an adventure and our future." She leaned her head against Evan's shoulder. "I'm ever so glad I did."

"I think all of us would agree," Cora Lee added, looking around the group before her gaze landed on Jace. The couple exchanged a private smile, one that made Cora Lee's cheeks turn pink.

Keeva remained quiet, which seemed so out of character for her, at least from what he knew about her. John couldn't help but want to ask her what was bothering her. What had dulled the sparkle of her personality? But it wasn't his place.

He was sure Evan and Henley were privy to whatever plagued her, but unless one of them sought him out, all he could do was pray for her as she journeyed onward, wherever that journey might lead.

John shouldn't, but he hoped that journey involved her remaining in Holiday.

Chapter Six

"If all you have is a sore throat, you don't need to see the doctor. Go home and make a nice hot cup of tea, stir in a big spoon of honey, and see if that doesn't help." Keeva leaned back in the chair at the desk in Evan's waiting room, doing her best to be helpful to the patients who came in to see her brother.

She'd had no idea how busy Evan and Henley were from early in the morning until late in the evening. In spite of Holiday being a small and relatively new community, Evan was the only doctor in the area, and people came from miles around seeking treatment.

With nothing to occupy her time beyond fixing meals, which Evan and Henley had gladly turned over to her, Keeva had offered to sit at the desk in the waiting room and keep track of patients.

At first, all she did was record their name, age, and ailment on a form and add it to a file. Or, if they already had a file, she got it out, ready to pass on to Henley since she was the one who escorted patients back to one of the examination rooms.

Due to the cramped quarters in Evan's home, Keeva had crammed her belongings in the recovery room in the clinic and slept on the narrow bed there. It was a far cry from her comfortable bed at home, but she had a roof over her head and wouldn't complain about cramped accommodations.

After witnessing the hectic pace at which Evan and Henley worked most days, Keeva decided she could help. Mam had taught her several easy home cures every woman should know, so she dispersed her knowledge and sent several patients on their way without having to bother her busy brother and sister-in-law.

"I'll give it a try, Miss Holt. Thank you." Mrs. Longbottom smiled at Keeva and left.

Before Keeva could do more than stand to stretch her muscles, another patient arrived. "Hello. How may we assist you today?" she asked, resuming her seat at the desk.

A man she gauged to be in his late forties held up a finger that sported a growth on the side of it. "Short of carving this thing off, I was wondering if Doc might have an idea of how to make it go away."

Keeva stood and leaned forward, studying what appeared to be a wart on the man's index finger. "My cousin had a wart just like that. My aunt soaked a piece of raw beef in vinegar, then each night she'd place a piece of the meat on the wart, wrap it with a bandage, and my cousin would sleep with it on. After three weeks, the wart went away."

The man's eyes widened. "Really? That's all I gotta do?"

"You can give it a try. If it doesn't work, you can always come back and have the doctor remove it."

"I'll try it. Any particular cut of meat?"

Keeva shook her head. "Stop by the butcher and get a few scraps. You need it to be meaty, though, not fat."

"Thank you, Miss. I'll—"

Henley strode into the room with a shocked expression on her face and stepped around the desk. "Perhaps you should let Doc take a look at that for you, Mr. Eldredge."

"Oh, I reckon I'll give this little gal's suggestion a try. Can't hurt nothing, can it?"

"I suppose not, but I really think it would be best if you let the doctor take a look at it."

As though she hadn't spoken, the man opened the door and tipped his hat. "I'm off to the butcher shop." He closed the door behind him as he left.

Without saying a word to Keeva, Henley disappeared down the hallway to the examination rooms. Keeva heard Evan speaking to the patient he'd been tending, a miner who'd cut his arm on one of the ore carts and required stitches.

Keeva mentally agreed he needed Evan's help in sewing the gash together and cleansing the wound, but there were many people spending their hard-earned money to see her brother when it wasn't necessary. Besides, Evan had more patients than he could handle most days. If Keeva could send some of them on their way, it seemed like a helpful way to address a growing problem.

She wanted to do all she could to help the people in town and also give Evan and Henley more time to rest. They worked far too hard to fulfill the needs of the area's sick and injured.

"Be sure you keep your arm wrapped and clean, Mr. Freeman. I'll come up to the mine to check on it next week if you don't stop in before then," Evan said, walking the miner to the door.

"Thanks, Doc. I appreciate your help."

"Of course. It's why I'm here. To help." Evan opened the door and waited until the miner was beyond the range of hearing to close the door and turn to Keeva with a withering glare.

"What?" Keeva asked, looking from him to Henley, who also appeared peeved although she had no idea why.

"Have you been dispersing Mam's ancient medical lore and chasing away my patients?" Evan asked in an accusatory tone.

Keeva took exception to his attitude. "It's not medical lore. They are proven methods that will save people money. They don't need to pay to have you look in their throat and tell them it's red. I merely told Mrs. Longbottom to try honey with her tea to ease her throat pain."

"And what about Mr. Eldredge? Did you give him Aunt Mirvena's loony cure for warts? Who in their right mind wants raw meat wrapped around their finger? Besides, it doesn't work. Cousin

Martin has more warts on his hands than an entire coven of witches have on their behi—"

Henley stepped in front of Evan, interrupting him. "I think what your brother is trying to say is the point of people coming here is for us to help them. Evan is a medically trained and experienced physician. He needs to assess the patients and decide on a course of treatment. It would be best if you would simply record their information, then ask them to wait until it is their turn."

Keeva sighed, realizing she'd overstepped—again. She'd all but taken over the kitchen in the house, which neither Henley nor Evan seemed to mind, but when she'd moved things around to suit herself, her brother had protested.

Throughout her growing up years, Evan was the sibling she'd always been the closest to. Now, though, he seemed to find her presence annoying.

Keeva wondered if she'd made a terrible mistake in coming to Holiday. Emotion swelled in her, along with tears. Lest they spill out and make her appear like a manipulative child, she turned and pretended to sort through a stack of files while attempting to get control of herself.

"Keeva," Evan said, in a much kinder, patient tone as he placed a hand on her shoulder. "I know this is a challenging situation for you. I know we've been busy and haven't had much time to make you feel welcome. I'm sorry for being short tempered. It's just that I …" Evan looked over at Henley, and she nodded, "we are used to doing things a certain way and that is truly how we prefer they be done."

"So, no more dispensing of Mam's home remedies?" Keeva asked, glancing over her shoulder at Evan with a small smile.

"Absolutely no more of her quackery." Evan lifted an eyebrow and waggled it. "If I hear you sharing any more of her atrocious cures, I shall sneak into your room after you fall asleep and wrap raw meat around your fingers and toes, then leave the door open for Tuesday to come nibble at you all night."

Keeva rolled her eyes. "Tuesday likes me. Besides, you'd never allow him into the clinic. Since I sleep in the recovery room, I'm safe."

"For now," Evan said, then glanced at the clock on the wall. "Come on, ladies. Let's take advantage of this rare peaceful moment and eat lunch. If we hurry, we can make it to the hotel dining room before they close for the afternoon."

"I can put something together, Evan," Keeva offered, but the idea of eating out held a great deal of appeal.

"My treat," Evan said, pushing down the shirt sleeves he'd rolled up earlier.

"Let's hurry, Keeva, before he changes his mind," Henley said with a smile. She grabbed Keeva's hand, and they hurried down the hall. It only took them a moment to freshen up. Evan waited for them in the living room, then they strolled out into the bright spring sunshine and made their way to the hotel. The lunch crowd had already dispersed, so the dining room was mostly empty.

Edith Piedmont waved as they took seats at a table in front of a window. She disappeared into the kitchen and returned with a tray that held three glasses of water.

"Good afternoon," she said as she set the glasses on their table.

"What are you doing waiting tables, Edith?" Evan asked as she stepped back.

"One of the waitresses left on the morning train. Her mother took sick, and she rushed off to be with her, not that I blame her."

"So, you're looking for a temporary helper, perhaps?" Henley inquired, looking hopefully at Keeva.

Aware of the direction the conversation was headed, Keeva brought it to an abrupt end. "Before you two suggest I apply for the job, you should know I'm terrible at waiting tables. I tried back home and quit after the second disastrous day. I can't keep the orders straight, and I can't seem to keep from visiting with people I know instead of bustling from one table to the next. I also dropped two entire trays full of dishes. As much as I admire you, Mrs. Piedmont, I feel I must make it clear you would be better off hiring Evan to help you than me."

The woman laughed. "That's alright, dear. We're all made to excel at different things. Now, what can I get you for lunch?"

They placed their orders. While they waited for their food, Keeva asked questions about residents of the town and some of the businesses she hadn't yet explored.

Edith set steaming pot pies on the table. They ate the tasty meals while continuing to talk about Holiday and job opportunities that might suit Keeva.

"It's too bad Edith doesn't need another cook. You'd do quite well at that," Evan mused as he leaned back in his chair after finishing the last bite of his meal.

"I might, but I don't fancy slaving away in a hot kitchen for hours and hours every day, Evan."

"What does tickle your fancy, little miss?" her brother asked in a teasing tone.

A vision of Pastor John Ryan popped into her head, but she certainly wouldn't give voice to that thought.

John had looked so handsome Sunday when he'd joined them for lunch at Elk Creek Ranch. Rather than wearing his stiff and proper suit, he'd dressed more like one of the ranch hands with denim pants, dusty boots, and a cotton shirt.

Mercy! He was a handsome man, with that chiseled jaw and square chin. A snub nose, full lips, and gorgeous blue eyes that made her feel like he could see all the way into her soul added to his attractive appearance.

Then there was his rich brown hair.

During the church service, it had been properly parted, and meticulously combed. But at the ranch, when he'd left off his hat and the breeze blew through it, thick waves broke free, tempting her fingers to run through them.

She almost laughed as she envisioned the horror that would appear on his face followed by a disapproving scowl if she did such a thing.

John Ryan might be a slightly rigid, somewhat stodgy pastor, but he was also an incredibly good-looking, virile young man. Keeva didn't think he could be more than twenty-five or twenty-six at the most. To her, that still seemed quite young, even if he acted much older.

His age, opinions, and anything else regarding the pastor really was none of her business. She had vowed to remain single all her days, and if that was going to happen, she needed to figure out some means of employment.

She obviously was not going to be able to work, even in a temporary position, as a secretary at Evan's clinic. Keeva had no idea what she could do, but there had to be some way for her to make an honest living.

Henley had cautioned her to stay away from the end of town where the saloons, particularly the notorious Ruby Palace, were located. The last thing Keeva wanted was to be accosted by a drunk or dragged into a dark alley.

Perhaps, if she walked around Holiday, though, making a list of the various shops and businesses, an idea would come to mind for something she could do for employment. Evan and Henley would graciously offer her room and board as long as she needed it, but they needed their own space without her interrupting what was clearly still part of their happy newlywed phase of life.

"Your fancy, Keeva? What strikes your fancy?" Evan asked again, jerking her from her musings.

She shrugged and dabbed at her lips with her napkin. "I can't honestly say, Evan. Other than working on the farm, and a failed attempt at being a waitress, I don't really have any skills."

"That's not true," Henley said, leaning forward and placing a hand on Keeva's arm. "You're so friendly and approachable. You're an excellent cook and know many domestic skills some people never learn. You're full of energy and fun. Those are all wonderful things, Keeva."

"Thank you, Henley. Unfortunately, I can't think of a single thing I can do with those skills to make money."

"Don't fret, Keeva. Something will come along. In the meantime, you're stuck with us," Evan said as he stood and left money on the table, then pulled out Henley's chair for her. "We should get back to the clinic."

"Would you mind if I take a walk around town?" Keeva asked as they walked out of the dining room.

Henley gave her a one-armed hug. "Take all the time you want to explore. It's much too pretty out today to be stuck inside a stuffy office anyway."

"Thank you." Keeva gave her sister-in-law a warm hug, wrinkled her nose at her brother, then tugged on her gloves and followed them out the door. "I might pick up a few things to make for supper. Any requests?"

"Colcannon soup and soda bread would sure hit the spot," Evan said, offering her a pleading look.

Keeva laughed. "You might think Mam's home remedies are quackery, but I see you still miss her cooking."

Evan shrugged. "Perhaps I do, from time to time. You're a grand cook yourself, Keeva. Mam taught you well."

"She did. I'll see you back at the house in a while."

"Enjoy your afternoon, Keeva. No hurry," Evan said, wrapping Henley's hand around his arm and heading off toward the clinic.

Keeva watched them walk away with a pain in her chest, knowing she'd never experience the kind of love Evan and Henley shared. It just wasn't meant to be. However, brooding over the fact wouldn't change anything.

With a determined step, she marched up the street, hoping an idea for gainful employment would soon present itself. If not, she might be forced to return to Pennsylvania and her family's farm. At least there, she didn't feel like an interfering interloper.

At home, she would be forever known as the jezebel who'd caused a fine young man to die.

Chapter Seven

"What are we going to do with her?" Evan asked Henley as they stood on the corner waiting for three wagons loaded with mine equipment to pass.

John had no doubt the *her* Evan referred to had to be his sister. He'd seen Evan and Henley walk by earlier with Keeva. Or was it Maureen? The girl seemed as inclined to change her name as she did her clothes. Which, by the number of pretty gowns he'd seen her wear, made him wonder if she'd brought trunks and trunks full of garments with her.

Not that he cared.

None of it was any of his business.

However, John couldn't help but overhear the doctor and his wife. After all, he'd been standing right behind them when Evan posed the question.

Henley shook her head, then glanced behind her, noticing John. She turned slightly and offered him a smile. "How does this day find you, John?"

"It finds me enjoying this beautiful day. How about the two of you?" Because he couldn't help himself, John took a step closer to the couple. "If I'm not mistaken, it sounds like you have a problem developing."

Evan sighed and rubbed a hand across the back of his neck. "It's just Keeva. She wants to help, but she is a little too ..." He paused and searched for the right word.

When it seemed he couldn't find it, Henley spoke up. "Ambitious, perhaps, might be the best word."

"Ambition doesn't seem like a bad thing. Or is it?" John asked, slightly confused. He had expected Evan to complain that Keeva wasn't trying to be helpful.

"Henley caught her dispensing her own medical advice to my patients and sending them on their way. It is pure nonsense passed from one well-meaning generation of women in my family to the next. None of it is harmful, but it isn't helpful either." Evan sighed again. "She wants to help, and her heart is certainly in the right place, but mostly she is underfoot."

"Oh, I see," John said although he didn't. It wasn't like Keeva was a child playing with her toys and leaving them scattered about the waiting room at the doctor's office. She was a grown woman attempting to offer assistance, even if her help was slightly misplaced.

"What will you do?"

"I have no idea," Evan said, appearing distraught. "We're so busy we do need the help, but Keeva and I working together is not a grand idea. We're—"

"Too much alike," Henley helpfully interjected, causing John to work to hide a grin.

Evan scowled at his wife, then looked at John. "I can't send her back home. Not after all she's endured. But she needs to find something to do that doesn't interfere with my medical practice."

"Is there anything I can do?" John asked.

"If you hear of anyone in need of help, let me know. Keeva's experience is mostly helping on my parents' farm, but she is a hard worker and intelligent. It wouldn't take her long to catch on to new tasks although she claims she is hopeless at waitressing."

John nodded slowly. "I did hear the Piedmonts were in need of temporary assistance. Did she check at the mercantile? Or perhaps someone might be willing to hire a nanny?"

"Other than a few of the mine owners, no one could afford to hire a nanny around here, and the last place Keeva needs to be is close to a mine. She'll find enough trouble here without placing her smack in the middle of it." Evan shook his head, looked across the street at the church, then slowly turned around. "What about you, John? You've mentioned you need help cleaning the church and keeping up with your appointments and whatnot. I'll even pay her wage if you give Keeva some work to do."

John took a step back and held up his hands like he was blocking an onslaught. "I don't think that would be a good idea. I have no idea what I'd have her do."

"She could clean the church and your house. Organize your appointments. Cook you a meal." Evan smacked his fist on the palm of his other hand. "That's it! Hire Keeva to be your housekeeper and cook, and to keep the church tidy. She could work for you from nine or ten until two or three. It would be a help to you and keep her out of my hair for a good part of the day."

John backed up another step, not sure where this conversation had taken such a wrong turn. He'd thought to offer a suggestion or two for Evan to be patient with his sister, and somehow the man and his wife now thought he should be the one to keep Keeva occupied. Honestly, they were all acting as though the girl—woman—had no say in what she wished to do.

"Please, John? Have mercy on me?" Evan pleaded with mock despair.

Henley smiled, then schooled her features into a serious expression. "What would it hurt to give it a try for a few days?"

John had no argument for that. It wasn't as if he could confess to Evan and Henley that he was incapable of keeping his eyes or thoughts off Keeva, despite his best intentions to ignore her vivacious presence. How would he maintain his sanity and resist the temptation she presented if she were flitting around him four or five hours a day?

On the other hand, he could use some help cleaning and organizing, and the thought of a midday meal he didn't have to fix held a great deal of appeal. He'd been meaning to clean the church from top to bottom and had put it off, waiting for some of the church ladies to organize a spring cleaning as they had in the past. However, there were things stored in the basement that needed to be sorted, like the Christmas play decorations and costumes. They'd discovered just before rehearsals began in December that mice had gnawed through half the costumes. Cora Lee and Anne had organized a group of women to quickly sew new ones.

He could set Keeva to cleaning. Part of the reason John didn't use the office at the church was because he'd never taken time to organize it. It was a nice space with a big desk Grant Coleman had donated, but it was a disorganized mess.

If Keeva set it to rights, he could meet with members of the congregation there instead of in the living area at his small house. Yes, he could see some benefits to having a helping hand.

He'd just have to be mindful of keeping his hands and thoughts in line when it came to the glorious girl.

"Fine. I'll give it a try, but on a temporary basis. She may come to the church tomorrow, any time after nine."

"She'll be there," Evan said with a broad grin, shaking John's hand with such enthusiasm it nearly rattled his teeth. "You won't regret it."

"I already do," he mumbled to himself as Evan escorted Henley across the street.

What had he just gotten himself into?

Chapter Eight

John slid both hands into his already disheveled hair and fought the urge to pull out a fistful. *That* woman was going to cause him to drink! At the very least, she'd give him enough distress he'd end up in a mental institution thinking a bag of marbles was his best friend.

In the short time she'd been working for him, she'd driven him loony. It wasn't any one thing in particular that had unsettled him, but everything. The first thing she'd done when she'd arrived the morning after he'd spoken with Evan and Henley was to stand on his doorstep at half past seven and pound on his door like the world was about to end.

He didn't know if he was more annoyed by how badly he wanted to whip off the cloth she'd tied over her shiny curls and let the sun glisten in her hair, or the fact that her loud raps on the door had come when he'd been in the process of shaving and he'd nicked his chin. After hastily wiping away his shaving soap, he'd shoved his arms into the sleeves of a shirt and yanked up his suspenders as he'd rushed to the door, thinking someone was in need of his services.

He'd opened it to find Keeva standing there, looking waifish with that ridiculous rag on her head and a smile on her face that warmed him far more than the burgeoning sunlight.

She'd spent the entire first day in the church. After she'd climbed a ladder she'd dragged up from the basement, she'd retrieved a broom and gone about the task of brushing down the steepled ceiling of the church.

John had tasks he needed to see to, but he'd feared the reckless woman would break her neck. Twice, he'd steadied the teetering ladder when she'd stood on the top rung, leaning as far as she dared in order to reach the high center of the ceiling. He tried to take the broom from her and do the work himself, but she'd threatened to swat him with it if he tried.

When he hadn't been checking to make sure her life wasn't in immediate peril, he'd attempted to work in his office. He quickly discovered not only was Keeva's presence a distraction, but so was her singing. She could carry a tune well enough, but it wasn't the quality of her singing, or even the song selection he found so diverting. It was the sultry tone of her voice that had plucked at every one of his nerves until he felt as though he was wound tighter than a twisted coil of rope.

DREAMS WITH FAITH

This morning, to John's great dismay, Keeva had invaded his office. She'd taken everything off his bookshelves, while sucking on a peppermint stick like she was a child instead of a grown woman. She'd gathered all the boxes he'd never gotten around to unpacking and carried them out into the church nave to get them out of the way, then set up the ladder to dust the ceiling. He'd watched out of the corner of his eye as she'd wiped down the walls in the room. She'd washed one of the two windows before she'd suddenly disappeared.

"Where has she gone off to?" he asked as he glanced at the clock for the fifth time in thirty minutes. He waited another twenty before he went in search of her. She wasn't anywhere in the church, so he walked over to his house, hungry and planning to prepare a sandwich for lunch.

He found her in his kitchen, cooking a meal. The food smelled different, nothing like what he was accustomed to eating. Already out of sorts from her turning the church into what appeared to be a disaster zone, he was appalled she'd wandered off without a thought of bringing order to the chaos.

He ate the meal she prepared with ingredients he didn't even know he had. There were rolls stuffed with sausage, cabbage, carrots, and spices. Keeva served potatoes mixed with egg and fried into patties until the outsides were golden brown and crisp and the insides were pillowy soft and tender. He might have complained about the strange combinations and flavors, except it all tasted so delicious. For dessert, she served a bowl of warm chocolate pudding. Much to his dismay, he actually groaned in delight as he took a second bite.

Keeva didn't sit with him as he ate. She'd cooked the pudding while he'd eaten the main course of the meal, then washed dishes while he devoured two bowls of pudding.

"You need to eat," he finally said, after wiping his mouth on a napkin.

"I brought a sandwich I ate earlier," she said over her shoulder and continued scrubbing pots and pans.

"If you plan to continue cooking lunch, you may as well eat with me, Miss Holt. It's ridiculous for you to pack a lunch."

She shrugged, as if it made no difference to her either way and continued washing the dishes.

John grabbed a towel and hastened to dry them, then helped Keeva put them away.

It wasn't until the third time he'd inadvertently bumped into her that he realized he had a problem. An enormous problem. And the problem's name was Maureen Keeva Holt.

Every time he drew near to her, all John wanted was to take her in his arms and hold her. To see if those rosy lips of hers would taste even half as sweet as they looked. To bury his hands in that unruly abundance of hair every bit as fiery as her personality.

He drew in a deep breath, hoping it would help calm him, and inhaled a lungful of her scent, something so feminine and alluring, he felt a tremor rock through him.

DREAMS WITH FAITH

"I have some people I need to visit," he said, tossing the dish towel on the edge of the sink and backing toward the door. "I'll see you later."

Like a coward, he grabbed his hat, shoved his arms into the sleeves of a light jacket, and raced outside.

John had no scheduled appointments, but he went to visit two elderly widows and stayed long enough to help with a few chores around their homes. He stopped to see an old man who was down with a case of gout. Then he checked in on the McBride family who had recently lost a baby. The poor little thing had gone to sleep and just never awakened.

Evan had been torn up over the death, wondering if there was something he could have done, but John knew it was just one of the things in life that happened without warning or explanation. God had plans for the baby, and John did his best to console the family with the thought the little one was in a better place no matter how much they missed their child.

He stayed for thirty minutes, sharing words of encouragement and praying with the family before he ventured over to the marshal's office.

Dillon was at his desk, writing reports, with the kitten he'd recently acquired for Zara curled into a fuzzy ball on the bed where Dillon still sometimes slept if he had a prisoner to guard in the jail. He glanced up with a welcoming smile when John sank onto a chair across from him.

"Why so glum?" Dillon asked as he leaned back in his chair. "I heard Miss Holt has been helping you the past few days. You ought to be thrilled someone is willing to clean up after a slob such as yourself."

"See here, now!" John glowered at his friend. "I may be many things, but a slob is not one of them."

Dillon chuckled and stood, walking over to the coffee pot that percolated on the stove. "I know, but it's fun to see you riled up for a change. I take it Miss Holt is still rattling your cage."

John glowered at him. "I never once said she rattled anything, and you know it."

Dillon poured two cups of coffee and handed one to John, then resumed his seat at his desk. "I know, but I got the idea when she was here last summer, you took quite a shine to her. Now that she's back for who knows how long, there's enough heat sizzling between you two to fry eggs and a side of bacon."

"There is not!" John denied vehemently.

Dillon took a long slurp of coffee, then looked over the rim at John. "You, of all people, ought to tell the truth, Pastor Ryan."

Convicted, John set the cup of coffee he held on Dillon's desk, dropped his hands to his lap and slowly nodded. "I know, Dill, I know. But that woman. She ... it's just that I ..." John sighed. He had no idea how to express his thoughts when they roiled and tumbled around in his head.

"It's okay, my friend. I understand. It wasn't all that long ago that I was in your shoes before I figured out the problem was that I loved Zara with my whole heart and nothing else mattered but being with her. Once I got that lined up in my head, everything else fell into place."

"I don't think I love Keeva. Maureen. Miss Holt. Whatever name she's picked today."

Dillon snickered. "She is a bit of a free spirit, that one. And beautiful. How old is she? I thought she was just a kid when her family came for Evan and Henley's wedding, but apparently, I was wrong."

"She just turned eighteen. Technically not a child, but she still has some growing up to do."

"I reckon that could be said about most of us who are younger than Mrs. Nordam."

John stared across the desk at Dillon. "She's got to be ninety if she's a day."

"Exactly." Dillon took another sip of coffee.

John picked up his cup and took a drink. Dillon might not cook any better than John could, but he did make a good pot of coffee.

"Any advice?" he finally asked his friend. After all, Dillon was older, generally wiser, and had talked a beautiful woman into marrying him last fall.

"Don't close your mind to any possibilities, and then follow your heart." Dillon offered him a pointed look. "I know Keeva is nothing like that list of requirements you've settled on for a suitable bride, but maybe she's God's way of telling you He has someone better in mind."

"Maybe." John realized the one thing he hadn't done was pray for clarity when it came to Keeva. It would behoove him to see to that right away.

Dillon leaned forward and set his cup on the desk. "You've prayed with me often enough these past years. Would you mind if I said a prayer for you?"

"I'd like that, Dill. Thank you." John bowed his head. Attentive, he listened to Dillon's heartfelt prayer and felt encouraged when his friend finished. He drained his cup of coffee, stood, and reached across the desk. "Thank you."

"Anytime, John. Anytime." Dillon shook his hand, then walked him to the door. "You'll still come for lunch Sunday, won't you?"

"I wouldn't miss it. I'll see you Sunday, if not before." John stepped outside, and Dillon followed.

"If you need a listening ear, you know where to find me."

"I do, and thanks."

John strode across the street and back to his house. He assumed Keeva was probably still in the church, creating more messes, so he entered through the back door, sank into his favorite chair, and opened his Bible, spending several hours deep in study.

Saturday morning, he expected Keeva would stay home, but he heard a crash from inside the church while he was scrambling eggs for his breakfast. He set the skillet on a folded towel and raced outside. Heart pounding, he took the church steps three at a time, skidding to a stop as he watched Keeva pick herself up off the floor. The overturned ladder rested beside her.

"Are you injured?" he asked, rushing to her and settling his hands on her arms. When he did, heat surged through his fingers and up his arms, making him feel like he'd grabbed onto a hot branding iron. After he helped her stand, he dropped his hands and took a big step back. Back from the temptation she represented with her bun sliding off the side of her head and curls escaping to frame her face. In an apron too big for her slender frame, and a dress the color of pink rose petals, she looked like a child playing dress up.

He knew she was no child, though. Not with curves that tugged at his interest and a beguiling smile that tested his power of resistance.

Seeking levity or at least something to distract them since she seemed to be as intensely aware of him as a man as he was of her as a woman, he grinned and took another step back. "If you are hurt, I know a doctor I can recommend."

Keeva grinned, as he'd hoped she would, and brushed at the back of her skirt. "I'm fine. I leaned too far on the ladder, and over it went. I'm sorry. I didn't mean to disturb you, Pastor Ryan. I wanted to finish cleaning the windows and get the church set back to rights before the service tomorrow."

At least she intended to pick up some of her messes. He'd stepped into the church last night to find an even bigger disaster both in his office and the nave. Rather than fuss and fume, he'd returned to his house and resumed reading his Bible. So far, he hadn't experienced an epiphany or revelation in regard to Keeva.

He did care about her, though. He'd even admit he was fascinated by her, but that wasn't necessarily a good thing. What he needed was to wait and listen for God's leading instead of letting his unsettling attraction to her pull him off kilter.

John set the ladder upright, nodded once at Keeva, then hurried back to his house.

After he'd eaten his breakfast, he decided the only way he'd get any peace was to distance himself from Keeva. He gathered a writing tablet and pencil, his Bible, and the notes he'd written for his sermon late last night when he found himself unable to sleep, and went for a walk. He sat on a stump at the edge of a meadow not far from town. He sometimes came here when he needed quiet and assurance he wouldn't be disturbed. Dillon knew where to find him if he wasn't in town, just like John knew to look for his friend by the river if he turned up absent when he was needed.

With a prayer for focus, John spent the morning writing and rewriting his sermon. Once he was satisfied with it, he recited it to a raccoon peeking at him from behind a tree, then walked back into town.

He stepped into the house to find Keeva humming as she worked in the kitchen. Her enchanting fragrance tickled his nose.

"Is that beef casserole?" he asked, setting his things on the desk in the living room, then moving into the kitchen.

"We call it cottage pie. It's something we make at home all the time. I got some beef from the butcher. Is that alright?"

John nodded. He had no idea how to prepare it himself, but he'd enjoyed the beef casseroles his mother had always made with vegetables and potatoes.

"It smells good," he said, stepping around her to wash his hands at the sink. As he dried them, Keeva set biscuits, butter, and a jar of jam on the table. It appeared she'd been busy in his absence, as evidenced by the pie she pulled from the oven and set to cool by an open window.

John sniffed and caught the aroma of sweet berries. She must have found a jar of canned huckleberries somewhere because it was the only purple fruit they had growing in abundance in the mountains around Holiday.

Thoughts of growing things reminded him he intended to plant a garden. R.C. Milton had kindly plowed a little plot behind the house last week. All John needed to do was work the dirt to soften it, hoe the rows, and plant the seeds and potatoes his sister-in-law had promised to send to him in her last letter.

John poured a glass of milk to go with his lunch and filled one for Keeva, then stood to the side as she set the steaming dish topped with slices of crispy potatoes on the table. "It looks wonderful, Keeva. Or is it Maureen? Or have you changed it yet again? Perhaps today you are Bethany or Bathsheba."

A blush filled her cheeks, and she turned away as she whipped off her apron, then plopped into the chair across the table from where he usually sat.

He moved to take a seat, aware of the heat still filling her face. "Have you changed your name to something else? Shall I call you Rose, since you seem to favor that color?"

The blush deepened to a shade of red. "Keeva will do just fine, Pastor Ryan."

"I see. Are you sure it isn't Maureen?" he teased.

"I think when I'm meeting someone I haven't met before, it would be proper to introduce myself as Maureen Holt. If they become a friend, they'll soon learn to call me Keeva. If they aren't more than an acquaintance, they may call me Maureen."

He couldn't argue with her logic, so he lifted the napkin from beside his plate onto his lap and bowed his head. After asking a blessing, he held out his plate, which Keeva filled since the serving dish sat nearest to her. She ladled two big scoops onto his plate before adding a small serving to hers.

"Would you like a biscuit?" he asked, holding the basket out to her.

She took a biscuit and began chatting about what a nice church building they had in Holiday, and how much she admired the simplicity of the design.

"The cross on top of the steeple is wonderful, like a promise stretching up to the heavens that our Heavenly Father will be honored here."

John stopped his fork halfway to his mouth, taken aback by Keeva's words. Maybe there was a bit of a poet lurking beneath her enchanting exterior. At the very least, she seemed to be acquainted with God's word.

"That's a wonderful way of thinking about it, Keeva. I appreciate you sharing that with me." He shoved the bite of savory beef and potatoes into his mouth, then forgot about the conversation as she talked. The dish was different than what his mother had made, but it reminded him of boyhood meals at the big table in their farmhouse.

"This is wonderful. Thank you," he said, shoveling in two more bites.

Keeva smiled. "If you like that, wait until you try the pie. I traded Mr. Rogers a dozen ginger cookies for the jar of berries. He said one of the women in town sells them in the autumn, and he buys as many as he can. It was one of his last jars."

"I'm sure the pie will taste delicious. Thank you." John wouldn't have minded sampling the cookies, but pie was a treat he didn't often eat. Just like the beef dish he couldn't seem to stop eating. After another serving of it and a second biscuit, he sat back, doubting he'd have room for the pie, but when Keeva sat a slice in front of him, he dove into it like he hadn't had a bite to eat in a month.

"So good," he muttered as he lifted another forkful of sweet berries and flaky crust to his mouth. If a man could get past Keeva's odd tendencies, like never finishing what she started, he'd be quite fortunate to marry her. Not only was she stunningly beautiful, but she was also a talented cook.

"Have you considered cooking as a career, Miss Holt?" John asked before he could swallow the words along with another bite of pie.

"No, I have not. I don't believe I'm cut out to cook in a hot kitchen for hours on end. I don't particularly enjoy cooking all that much although I am proficient in the skill. However, I do love to bake."

Thoughts of a bakery popped into his head. It would give Keeva a purpose and the town a much-needed business. The mercantile carried a few things, like bread baked by one of the widows, and desserts were sold at the hotel. They were good, but nothing like the treats Keeva created.

However, it would take an investment to start a business, and he knew Keeva didn't have the funding. Perhaps Evan would give her a loan, but that seemed like a lot to ask of the doctor.

John forked another bite of the pie. "You have a talent for baking. This is one of the tastiest pies I've ever eaten."

"Thank you," she said, then hopped up and began washing dishes. John finished his slice of pie, looking forward to eating more of it later, set his dirty dishes in the sink, then retreated to the living room to his desk to review the hymns he'd selected for the service tomorrow.

The clank of dishes quieted, and he heard the back door open and then click shut. A glance out the side window let him know Keeva returned to the church as he watched her race up the steps. He hoped she left early today so he'd have time to clear out her cleaning supplies, shove the boxes from his office back into the corner they had occupied since he'd moved to town, and prepare the church for tomorrow.

No more loud bangs or crashes trailed through his open windows, but he did spy Keeva outside on the ladder with a bucket and rag, cleaning the windows. When she finished, she swept the front steps until he was sure she'd wear grooves through the wood.

Just when he thought he couldn't stand to stay away a moment longer, she bounded down the steps, waved toward the window where he peered out at her, and hurried on her way.

Embarrassed to have been caught observing her, he jerked back inside, once again smacking his head on the window.

With a hand rubbing the spot still tender from hitting the window when Keeva had first arrived in town, he muttered to himself about well-meaning menaces as he marched outside and up the church steps. He stopped to admire how nice the building looked with the windows gleaming and not a speck of dust lingering on the steps. Keeva had even polished the wood of the door as well as the knob.

He turned it and stepped inside, expecting to see the ladder, her cleaning supplies, and his boxes of files and books strewn everywhere. Shocked, he stepped further into the church, admiring the glistening windows, the gleaming floor, and polished pews. Keeva had scrubbed and cleaned and dusted until the entire building shone. The fresh, clean smell didn't pass his notice either.

John drew in a deeper breath, catching the faintest hint of Keeva's soft fragrance. Irritated with himself for noticing it, he rubbed a finger beneath his nose and made his way down the center aisle to the pulpit. The wood gleamed, as did the piano in the corner.

He had no idea how she'd accomplished so much in so little time. The past few days, it seemed to him she hadn't managed to do anything but create a disorderly mess. But perhaps she'd been cleaning all the while and the things that were out of place distracted him to the point he missed all she had done.

Uncertain what to think, he made his way to his office, half expecting to find the ladder on the floor, but it was as clean as the rest of the building. All the boxes he'd stuffed in the corner were gone, and a comfortable chair with a small end table and a globe lamp filled the space. He had no idea where she'd found the pieces of furniture. They didn't appear new, but they still had plenty of wear left in them.

His books were arranged alphabetically on the shelves, along with a few mementoes he'd half-forgotten he'd even brought to Holiday. He picked up a wooden cross his grandfather had carved for him and smiled, thinking how much Grandpa would have liked Keeva. He always said spunk and gumption went farther than good intentions that never happened.

Keeva had more spunk than anyone John had ever encountered. Far too much for a meek and humble pastor's wife.

John shook his head. Why did every thought of Keeva bring him back around to his longing for a wife? She just simply wouldn't do. She needed a man as full of energy and spirit as she possessed, not someone like John who was quiet and reserved.

He briefly considered Rowan Reed. The rancher hadn't been in the area all that long, and he mostly kept to himself, although he did attend church with some regularity. The man wasn't bad to look at, dressed well, carried himself with confidence, and would make a more suitable husband for Keeva than John ever could.

Perhaps tomorrow after the service, he'd make sure the two of them were introduced if they hadn't yet been.

Yes, that was just the ticket.

He'd find Keeva a husband, then he would have no choice but to push her out of his thoughts for good and get back to his search for his ideal wife.

Chapter Nine

"That man is an unmitigated, undeniable, unbelievable idiot!" Keeva slammed the door behind her, making Evan's cat howl and leap for the open kitchen window. "See what he made me do. I'm sorry, Tuesday!" she yelled after the cat that had already jumped out the window.

"May we assume you're referring to the pastor?" Henley asked in a calm, patient voice as she lifted a roasting pan out of the oven Keeva had slid in earlier that morning. Cora Lee had been giving Henley cooking lessons throughout the winter, and Henley was gaining skills, but she still had a way to go. Keeva was more than happy to feel useful by preparing their meals.

The scent of roasted chicken mingled with the mouth-watering aroma of yeasty rolls Keeva had prepared earlier that morning. Henley slid half a dozen of them into the oven to warm, then got out three plates to set the table.

Keeva yanked off her hat and yelped when she realized she'd forgotten to remove the pin holding it in place. It helped not a whit that Evan struggled to hide his humor behind a feigned cough.

Frustrated with herself and especially John Ryan, she stamped both feet then pulled out the hatpin, removed her hat, and gave it a fling. It sailed across the room and landed on the floor by Evan's favorite chair.

He raised an eyebrow and stepped around the couch, giving her a look filled with understanding instead of the censure she'd expected and rightfully deserved. She'd lost her temper, and now that it was loose, it was hard to cram it back into the locked box where she tried to keep it.

Evan understood, though, because he had the same temper, inherited from their mother. He placed a hand on her shoulder and lowered his voice to a soothing tone. "Take a deep breath, Keeva. Breathe in."

She did as he directed.

"Now, let it go. The breath and your temper. Let it flow out."

Keeva blew out the breath and felt marginally better. She drew in half a dozen more and released them before she felt capable of speaking without yelling. Or throwing things. Or throwing things while yelling.

By the time she'd changed into a plain pink cotton dress and washed her hands, she once again felt reasonably calm.

Henley, with Evan's assistance, finished dishing up the meal and had everything on the table when Keeva returned to the kitchen.

She gave them both sheepish looks. "I apologize for roaring into the house like a summer storm."

Evan winked at her. "You're forgiven if you tell us what John did to irk you so."

Keeva sank into the chair next to Henley and folded her hands in her lap. "I will after you ask the blessing."

Evan bowed his head and asked a blessing on their meal and offered a word of thanks for the bounty they received each day. When he asked the Father to guide them through the coming week, Keeva felt in desperate need of divine guidance.

While her brother carved the chicken, Keeva took a moment to offer her own silent prayers of gratitude and sought the Lord's leading for her life because she'd certainly made a mangled mess of things on her own.

Once their plates were filled, Evan took a bite of the tender chicken, nodded in approval, then pointed at Keeva with his fork. "Now, spill it all, little sister. What did John do to make you so angry?"

Keeva felt her ire building just recalling what the pastor had done. "After I told you I'd walk home later since I was holding baby Charles and wasn't ready to let him go, I visited with Anne and R.C. Then I realized most everyone had gone, so I handed back the baby. While the last few people greeted the pastor, I decided to do a little straightening. You know there are always a few things to pick up after everyone has been at the service. Anyway, I was bent over retrieving a pencil stub from beneath one of the pews when the pastor cleared his throat from right behind me. It startled me so thoroughly, I whomped my head on the pew, tripped on the hem of my skirt, and would have fallen right on my face if John, I mean the pastor, hadn't caught me."

Angry all over again, Keeva jabbed her fork into her mashed potatoes and twirled it around with enough force potatoes flew off her plate, plopping all over the table.

Evan gently pried the fork from her fingers. Keeva sighed, placing her hands in her lap and again listening as her brother helped her take several calming breaths.

Henley settled her hand on Keeva's shoulder and patted it gently. "Did something happen? Do we need to speak to the pastor?"

Keeva shook her head as her cheeks warmed with the embarrassment she'd felt earlier but had been too livid to acknowledge. In truth, she'd nearly given in to her desire to rant like an enraged cavedweller.

"The pastor wasn't alone. He had Rowan Reed with him." Keeva's cheeks burned with embarrassment all over again. "It seemed he intended to encourage us to spend time together. There isn't a doubt in my mind that meddling idiot thinks he's playing matchmaker, and I won't stand for it! I just won't!"

Her voice echoed off the walls, and she shot Henley an apologetic look, only to find the woman doing her best to hide a grin.

"It's not funny!"

Evan smirked. "It rather is, Keeva. John has been smitten with you since you came to visit last summer. You are clearly enamored with him. How long will it take the two of you to figure it out?"

"What nonsense are you spewing, Evan?" Keeva pushed back from the table. "I believe I'm no longer hungry."

"Keeva. Stop." Evan grabbed her wrist before she could hop up and storm from the room. "Whatever happens between you and John is your business, not mine. You are an adult and capable of making your own choices. But just give some thought as to why he might be introducing you to Mr. Reed. I think John is as reluctant to admit he's in love as you are. That's all. He's not intentionally trying to test your patience, which clearly is at an end. Come now. Eat this fine lunch you've worked so hard to prepare. This afternoon will be time enough to sit and contemplate how painfully dense John is behaving."

The tiniest beginnings of a smile pulled at Keeva's lips. "He is painfully dense, and positively tiresome."

Henley gave her an encouraging smile, then looked at Evan. "Wasn't the song Anne and Jace sang this morning beautiful? Sometimes, the way those two can harmonize makes me wonder how lovely a heavenly choir will sound."

Keeva was grateful for the change of topic and managed to eat her lunch without erupting into more fits of fury. By the time she served the cake she'd baked with generous dollops of fresh cream on each plate, she'd calmed considerably.

"This cake is even better than Mam makes, Keeva," Evan gushed as he helped himself to a second slice. "I know you don't want to work as a waitress or a cook at the hotel, but you should ask Edith if she'd purchase baked goods from you. The cook they have makes passable desserts, but they are nothing like you create."

Keeva looked at Evan to see if he was serious. Assured that he was by the ravenous manner in which he shoveled in one bite of cake after another, she decided he wasn't teasing her but was utterly serious.

"I might just do that. Do you have something in mind you think I should bake for a sample?"

"Your apple cake, or the chocolate potato cake. Those ginger cookies you made yesterday were delicious. Or some of the hand pies filled with pudding. Maybe you should make them all again so I can taste them and choose the best."

Henley rolled her eyes.

Keeva laughed, then gave Evan a playful shove. "Gluttony does not suit you, brother dear."

Evan shrugged and ate the last bite of his cake. "I'm stuffed and ready for a nap. I'll help with the dishes, then I'm going to see if I can catch an hour or two of rest."

"You go on. Henley too. You both were up half the night setting a broken leg for that man at the lumber mill." Keeva rose from the table and pulled on one of the aprons hanging on a hook near the sink. "I'm more than capable of seeing to the dishes. However, would anyone complain if we have sandwiches made with the leftover rolls and the ham from last night for our supper?"

"That sounds fine to me, Keeva." Henley smiled as she rose from the table, stretched, and yawned. "I am tired."

Keeva made a shooing motion toward their bedroom door. "It will just take a minute to do the dishes, then I think I'll take a walk. It's such a lovely afternoon."

"That it is. Just stay away from the pastor until you can talk to him without wanting to wallop him," Evan teased as he removed his tie on the way to the bedroom.

"Hmph!"

Keeva hurried to wash the dishes and put away the leftover food. Tuesday reappeared and she gave him a few pieces of chicken along with several scratches behind his ears before she quietly left and meandered down the street. She had no direction in mind, but she ended up wandering all the way out to the Milton place. She knew Anne and R.C. had gone out to Elk Creek Ranch for lunch, as they tended to do most Sundays.

With no place she needed to be, Keeva turned and wandered along Main Street, passing slowly by each business. She looked in shop windows although everyone was closed on Sunday. A pair of gloves caught her eye in the mercantile window, and she admired them before continuing on her way. The streets were all but abandoned, and she'd seen nary a soul out to talk to. She debated on where to go to give Henley and Evan more time to rest as she stood on the corner across the street from the church.

Was Evan correct? Did she love John? Did he love her?

Keeva thought she'd been in love with Oliver and Matthew, but what she felt for John was so different. So much deeper and broader and richer. Her feelings for him felt complex and yet simple, because if she cared to admit it, she did love him. She realized she'd loved him since the first moment she'd laid eyes on him last summer. Before she comprehended he was the pastor of the church, she'd thought he was the most handsome man she'd ever seen.

She still thought that even if he was her current pastor.

Did he truly care about her? If so, why did he work so hard to treat her with such polite indifference?

Perhaps he thought they were ill-suited for one another. He wouldn't be wrong. Keeva knew she was young and could be a bit flighty or brash, but she was trying to do better.

She was aware her methods of cleaning the church and organizing John's office had tested his patience, but just because she'd done things in a way different than he was used to didn't mean it was wrong. The end result was the same. The church had fairly sparkled during the service that morning. Additionally, John's office was organized, tidy, and welcoming.

The chaos she'd found there clarified why he preferred to use the desk in his house than spend time in the church office. She hoped now, especially after she'd gotten the chair, table, and lamp from Mrs. Busby, that John would feel comfortable in the office space.

A man in his position needed an office where he could meet with members of the congregation, work on his sermons, or sit in peaceful solitude if the mood struck him.

Keeva tried to picture herself as a docile pastor's wife and nearly laughed aloud at the notion. She didn't possess a docile, unassuming, or timid bone in her body. Often, she forged ahead without assessing the entire situation, and she probably shared her opinions more freely than she should, but she wouldn't apologize for being herself.

If John expected her to, he'd wait a long, long time before that ever happened.

As though thinking about John made him materialize, she felt his presence beside her before she turned and looked at him.

"Where did you come from?" she asked, looking away because John appeared so handsome in his Sunday suit.

"I had lunch with the marshal and his wife at his grandmother's place. Well, Nan is his adopted grandmother, but they are family even if they aren't related by blood. It's not far out of town, so I walked. I just happened to see you standing here. Is everything alright?"

Keeva nodded, not trusting herself to look at him. "Everything is perfectly fine."

"Look, Keeva, about earlier. I didn't mean to … that's to say, I wasn't trying … I shouldn't have …"

She turned to face him when his voice trailed off. "If that's your way of apologizing for attempting to foist me onto Mr. Reed, apology accepted."

John appeared relieved. "I really am sorry, Keeva. I've already apologized to Rowan. He made it understood he was not interested in taking on a wife and would skip church if I intended to try something like that again."

"Then I suppose you learned your lesson," Keeva said, taking a step closer to John and brushing a bit of lint from his shoulder. "My father says mistakes are just lessons in the making."

His hands slid around her waist, and it felt like the most natural thing in the world when he pulled her close to him. She felt his forehead rest against hers for a sweet moment as they remained unmoving, learning how delightful—how incredibly right—it felt to be held in the circle of his arms.

Slowly, John's head dipped lower until his lips brushed hers in a light, sweet kiss.

"John," she whispered, not certain what she wanted from him. The only thought in her mind was more. She wanted more kisses. More hugs. More moments like this where all the world seemed to disappear until nothing remained except the two of them.

"Maureen Keeva Holt," he whispered against her hair. "What have you done to me?"

She had no answer for him. Couldn't think with his hands caressing her waist and the spicy, earthy smell of him tantalizing her nose. His warmth surrounded her, and she knew that Evan was right. She loved John. Loved him deeply and passionately.

She wanted him. Not just for a moment, or a few stolen kisses, but forever.

And that seemed an impossible dream. She'd dreamed of John many times, starting when she'd met him last summer. He'd been in her dreams with growing frequency since then. But that's all they were. Dreams of a girl that would never come true.

"Keeva. I care about you, I truly do. But as much as I'd like to court you, this will never work between us. We're just too—"

"Different." Keeva sighed and took a step back. "You wouldn't ever want someone like me, Pastor Ryan. I know that. I don't think it would be a good idea for me to continue to help at the church or make your meals. I should go."

She turned to leave, but John grabbed her arm and tugged her around. Unexpectedly, he kissed her with all the yearning and longing and hunger she'd felt since the moment he'd smiled and said hello to her last year. When he let her go, she lifted her skirts and ran back to Evan's place.

Desperate to escape her feelings and in need of time to herself to think things through, she hastily packed a bag, filled a basket with food, wrote Evan and Henley a note and set it beneath the sugar bowl on the table, then ran to the livery.

R.C. was just putting away his horse and buggy when she reached him, panting from the exertion of dashing through town.

"Is something wrong, Keeva? Is someone hurt?" R.C. asked, rushing over to her.

Other than her broken heart?

"No. Everyone is well, but might I borrow Evan's horse to ride up to his cabin?"

"Sure thing, Keeva. It will just take a minute to saddle him."

R.C. quickly saddled the horse and gave her a boost to mount him. After she settled her skirts, he handed her the bag and basket. "Are you sure you are well, Keeva?"

"I will be, but thank you." Without another word, she kicked the sides of the horse and rode through town.

She hadn't been to the cabin since last summer, but she remembered the way. Evan had added a small barn, where she left the saddle, brushed down Cauldron, filled a bucket with water and another with the feed Evan kept in a box in the barn, then carried her things into the cabin.

There was wood piled by the stove and stacked in the fireplace, ready to light a fire. The lamps were full, and there were even several candles in a box on a shelf. Keeva found canned goods in a cupboard and knew she would be fine for a few or several days. She'd brought sourdough starter in a jar as well as flour, tea, sugar, and bacon. Between those supplies and the canned goods, she certainly wouldn't starve. It wasn't as if it was a long ride into town. If she were of a mind to, she could have walked. At any rate, she intended to stay at the cabin until she figured out what to do with herself.

What she really wanted to do was ride back into town, pound on John's door until he opened it, then kiss him until he realized it didn't matter if they were different or exactly the same. What was important was that she loved him, and she was certain he loved her.

Not that it mattered now.

With her dreams as shattered as her heart, Keeva fell across the bed and let her pent-up tears work free.

Chapter Ten

John looked at the faces of his congregation, not surprised to see Evan, Henley, and Keeva absent.

The past week had been torturous for John. He'd replayed those moments he'd spent alone with Keeva over and over in his thoughts until he thought he might go completely mad.

He should never have kissed her in the first place, and absolutely shouldn't have plundered her sweet, delectable mouth a second time.

If he let go of his thoughts about what he required in a suitable wife and just let himself feel, he knew he'd never find anyone he loved more than Keeva.

What would people think? What would they say? How would they react to a pastor whose wife was so vibrant and full of life? To him, Keeva was like having sunbeams, stars, and moonlight all rolled into one glorious being.

She was more like a fanciful fairy than a serious, docile woman. Likely, she would never change, and he couldn't bring himself to wish she would.

He certainly couldn't fault her domestic skills. She had cleaned and organized the church more thoroughly than he'd imagined her capable. She'd tidied his home, prepared delicious meals, and proved to be a fascinating conversationalist.

John couldn't help but wonder how quickly he'd grow weary of and bored with a timid, somber woman. He was solemn enough without compounding the problem.

What if the person he needed was full of laughter and light? A person like Keeva?

Not someone like her, but Keeva.

Determined to seek God's direction once again instead of blundering ahead, John forced his attention back to the service and his sermon. He'd chosen the topic of brotherly love. Even as he said the words he'd carefully prepared to share, all that resonated in his thoughts was love.

Love, love, love.

The love he held in his heart for Keeva. He could deny it, but that would be lying. He'd realized during the past quiet, lonely week, he loved Keeva, and he missed her. He missed her smile and her laughter. He missed the spring in her step and the enthusiastic way she approached life. He'd missed her cooking, and how clean and fresh his home smelled after she'd been there.

What he really missed, though, was her. Missed the feeling of completeness he experienced when she was near.

John loved Keeva. Deeply. Yet, he still hesitated. Was he following God's plans for him or pursuing his own path? Was he dreaming selfish dreams when they centered on Keeva, or dreaming with faith?

Unable to answer the questions, he had no idea how to resolve them but to wait. He dragged his thoughts back to the present, wrapped up his sermon ahead of time, and, after a hymn and brief closing prayer, bid the congregation a good week ahead.

He thought the line of people leaving would never end as he shook one hand after another. When R.C. and Anne Milton faced him, he leaned closer to them, aware R.C. kept tabs on Evan's whereabouts a good deal of the time. "Was Evan called away this morning?"

"I haven't heard, but I assume he and Henley must be out on a call or they'd be here."

John nodded, unable to ask about Keeva. He couldn't blame her for staying away. He'd certainly not given her a reason to want to see him again. Not after telling her things between them would never work.

Did he know that for a fact? Was it a certainty?

No, it was not.

To make matters worse, Mrs. Lymon cornered him, demanding he join her and her little ruffian children for lunch. He made a flimsy excuse of not feeling well, which wasn't entirely untrue. John's stomach ached, like he'd swallowed rocks along with his eggs for breakfast.

By the time the last person left and he trudged to his house, he considered returning to bed and hoping he'd be in a better frame of mind when he awakened. He was grateful to not have any invitations for lunch today other than Mrs. Lymon's because he needed time to sort through his tumultuous thoughts.

By Thursday, he had a headache to accompany the stomachache and wondered if he was coming down with something.

Or perhaps, he was merely lovesick.

All he knew was that he missed Keeva. He needed her. He loved her.

He concluded he didn't care what others might think of the woman he married. That was his choice, and not theirs. If they were that judgmental, they had bigger problems than looking down their nose at his wife.

After spending hours on his knees in prayer, John kept hearing the same nudging whisper.

Talk to Keeva.

He had no idea what to say to her. Or if she'd even speak to him. But he decided he had to try. Either that, or he might end up needing to seek Evan's help for his increasing ailments. At the rate he was going he'd be ancient and withered by the time summer arrived.

John hadn't seen any of the Holts since the Sunday he'd kissed Keeva, which was odd. He normally saw Evan or Henley around town. Of course, he hadn't seen Keeva either although he'd been watching for her every time he'd stepped outside his door.

He'd even taken a walk around Holiday earlier, hoping to catch a glimpse of her.

Filled with a purpose, along with a measure of fear that Keeva would send him away, he walked to Evan's clinic and opened the door to the waiting room. Miraculously, it was empty, but he could hear voices coming from one of the examination rooms down the hall. Most likely, Evan and Henley were with a patient.

John settled onto one of the chairs, closed his eyes, and opened his heart, but there was that whisper in his thoughts again.

Talk to Keeva.

Five minutes passed, then ten. Just when John thought he might explode with impatience, Henley walked into the room with a miner who looked as though he'd been in a fight. He had a black eye, a split bottom lip, a splint on his left leg, and a sling holding his left arm against his chest.

"Howdy, Pastor. This is what happens when you fall down a mine shaft," the man said, offering him a lopsided, pain-filled grin that looked more like a grimace. "It was sure nice the last time you came out to the mine and offered a sermon. Think you might do that again?"

"I will, Mr. Sherman. I will definitely do that. You take care and be careful," John said, hopping up to open the door so the man could exit.

When he was gone and John had closed the door, Henley gave him a pointed look. "She's not here."

John could have feigned ignorance, but that wasn't his way. "Not here?" he asked, wondering where on earth Keeva could be. That red hair of hers was hard to miss, so he knew she wasn't anywhere in town. He'd looked.

"She's gone," Evan said, walking in the room and moving to stand with his hand on the curve of Henley's waist. Such a simple, yet entirely possessive gesture. One John wanted to have the right to share with Keeva.

"Gone?" John felt like a simpleton as he waited for his brain to engage. Had Keeva returned to Pennsylvania? If she had, John would go after her. He'd been saving his money to visit his family in September, but he'd spend every dime he had if that's what it cost to travel across the country and talk to Keeva.

"She's been staying at our cabin," Evan said, observing him.

A relieved breath whooshed out of John. "That's good."

Henley smiled. "She might even be so lonesome by now she'd welcome your company. We spent Sunday there with her and took up supplies."

"I see," John said, and he did. He understood why Evan and Henley would spend the day with Keeva instead of attending church. He understood why Keeva had likely refused to set foot inside the church where John presided. What he didn't understand was what he could do to set things right between him and the woman he loved.

DREAMS WITH FAITH

Henley moved forward and placed a hand on his arm, then smiled at him. "Go to her, John. Talk to her. If the two of you actually have an earnest conversation, you may be surprised what you learn."

John grinned and backed toward the door. "I'll do that. Right now."

"Go get your horse from R.C. For heaven's sake, man, don't run the whole way," Evan called after him when he started running down the street.

John lifted a hand to let the doctor know he'd heard then continued to his home. He changed into a pair of denims, a cotton work shirt, and a pair of boots. He didn't bother with a hat or vest. He stuffed a few coins in his pocket and hastened outside, stopping just long enough to pluck a bouquet of flowers from those blooming around his porch and outside the church.

With the flowers in hand, he raced through town, skidding to a stop at the livery.

"Is someone hurt? Do you need any help?" R.C. questioned as he hurried over, wiping his hands on a rag.

"I just need my horse," John said, bent over slightly to catch his breath. Apparently, he needed to include more physical exercise in his days if a fast-paced run through Holiday left him winded. "I'm riding up to Evan's cabin."

"It's about time," R.C. said, then grinned. "I heard Keeva has been hiding up there for a while. It's sure a pretty place."

"It is," John agreed, having been one of the men who helped build the cabin last summer.

It didn't take long for R.C. to saddle Esau for him and hand John the reins.

"I will have him back later today."

"No rush, John. Enjoy the ride and I hope things go well with Keeva."

John swung into the saddle. "I hope that very thing too."

He clucked to the horse and took off down the street. By the time they hit the outskirts of town, Esau stretched his long legs into a gallop. The scenery flew by as John rode out to the lake and up to the cabin where Keeva was staying. Cauldron, Evan's horse, peeked around the end of the barn and whinnied. He was probably lonesome and happy to see Esau since Evan kept the horse at the livery.

After seeing to his mount, John glanced down at the scruffy flowers and considered tossing them but decided to take them to Keeva anyway.

He tapped on the door of the cabin, but no one answered.

"Keeva?" he called, turning the knob and stepping inside. The cabin was well-constructed, and Henley had made it feel homey with curtains at the windows and fluffy pillows on the couch.

The scent of cinnamon hung heavy in the air along with something yeasty.

John's stomach growled at the fragrance floating around him. It was the first time he'd been hungry since he'd kissed Keeva and then bungled things with her so badly.

He turned and went outside, then glanced around. Keeva was down at the edge of the lake where it appeared she was doing a bit of washing.

Her hair hung down and loose in an explosion of riotous curls the sunlight turned aflame. She wore only a white chemise and bloomers as she bent over scrubbing what appeared to be one of her dresses on a small washboard.

The proper thing to do would have been for him to turn away and leave.

But John had no interest in being proper. Not now.

Not when he was so thoroughly in love.

With purposeful strides, he walked down the hill to the lake along a path, skirted around rocks, and didn't stop until he stood a few feet away from Keeva.

She was so lovely, the sight of her stole his breath. It felt like all the air evaporated from inside his lungs. Between her thick mass of tangled, slightly damp curls, the sunlight gilding her bare skin with gold, the feminine scent of her, and that sultry voice of hers humming a tune, John's legs quivered.

"Keeva," he said softly, hoping he wouldn't startle her. He wondered how she hadn't heard him approach. He made more noise than a bear chasing after a honeybee, but she jumped and sucked in a gasp while rising to her feet. She held the washboard out like a weapon, then recognition set in, and she lowered it.

He could see her chemise was damp, clinging to her in spots he should have averted his eyes from looking at, but he couldn't stop himself. She was just too beautiful to ignore.

"What are you doing here, Pastor Ryan?" she asked, dropping the washboard into the bucket of soapy water, then protectively crossing her arms over her chest.

"I came to see you." He held the flowers out to her, and she reluctantly took them. He felt encouraged when she buried her nose in the bedraggled blooms.

She glanced up at him, still appearing uncertain and slightly wary. Her eyes widened when John closed the distance between the two of them until all that was between them were the flowers and a few inches of space.

"What do you think you're doing?" she asked, trying to pull away from him. "This is highly improper, as you well know."

John inched closer to her. "I don't care, Keeva. I don't care what is proper or not. I don't care what anyone else thinks. I don't care if you decide to go by Maureen, or Keeva, or Hortense."

She wrinkled her nose. "Never Hortense."

He smiled. "The only thing I care about right now is you. About telling you the truth."

"And what might the truth be?" she asked quietly, trailing her fingers over the soft petal of a yellow tulip.

"That I love you, Keeva. I've loved you since the first day we met, and I will go on loving you until the Father calls me home. I've been in misery since you ran off because I miss you. I miss your humming. I miss your unorganized manner of approaching things but then accomplishing more than I could ever anticipate or expect. I miss your cooking and laughter and smiles. I miss the way your nose wrinkles up on the end when you grin, and how your freckles sprinkle your cheeks like they'd been dusted by a mischievous fairy. I miss the light flashing in your eyes and the sun dancing through your hair. I miss the soft fragrance of you. What I really miss, though, Keeva, is the joy you bring to my life, and the warmth you pour into my heart. Please come back to Holiday. Come home."

"I don't have a home, John. I'm a bothersome pest to Evan and Henley. I couldn't seem to do anything to please you. I have no real skills, although Edith Piedmont has agreed to purchase baked goods from me for the restaurant, so at least I'll have some meaningful employment." Keeva sighed and kept her gaze fastened to the flowers she held. "I missed you, too, you dense man. I've loved you from the first time I saw you right here at this cabin last summer. It has nothing to do with your incredibly good looks, though that doesn't hurt a thing. I miss you, John. You make me think, cause me to see things in a different manner than I might have, and you challenge me to be a better person. Not only that, but you make my heart full and happy, and there is nothing I'd like better than to be able to freely love you, but you said it yourself. We're just too different."

John shook his head and pulled Keeva into his arms, smashing the flowers between them. "I'm an idiot and a dunce, Keeva. I've been praying and praying for clarity about what to do, and the only thing I could hear was a whisper telling me to come talk to you. So, I'm here. Talking to you when I'd much rather be kissing you. I think, Maureen Keeva Holt, you should marry me. Like every other married couple, we'll figure things out as we go. We are different, but that doesn't mean we aren't well suited for each other. In fact, I can't think of anyone better suited to be my wife than you. I don't want anyone but you. I know I can be a bit set in my ways and …"

At his pause, Keeva grinned, dropped the bouquet, and wrapped her arms around his neck, removing the last bit of space between them. "You can be as fussy as a finicky old maid, but I love you anyway, John Ryan. I love you with all my heart. I know I'm young and have a lot to learn, but I'll do my best to try to make you proud."

Again, he gave his head a shake. "No, Keeva. You don't need to work to make me proud. You already do. Don't change who you are. Just grow into who God wants you to be. I love who you are today, who you'll be tomorrow, and the person you'll be fifty years from now. No matter what, it's still going to be you that I love. What I'd like, more than anything, is the privilege of growing old with you. Will you marry me, Keeva? Would you consider becoming a pastor's wife?"

"I will consider it." She pulled away from him slightly, tapped a finger to her chin and fastened her bright green gaze on the sky, then smiled and entwined her fingers around the back of his neck. "After due consideration, my answer is yes. I will marry you, John Ryan. I'll be your wife and partner, and walk through this life's journey with you."

"Then I think we need to seal that promise with a kiss," he said in a husky voice he hardly recognized as his own.

With his hands bracketing Keeva's waist, he lowered his head, and their lips met in a tender exchange that soon gave way to something heated that pulsed with longing.

John broke away and stepped back. "Before things get carried away, you best put on your clothes. What do you say to coming back to Holiday with me and getting started on our future plans?"

"I'd say that's a brilliant idea, Pastor Ryan." Keeva kissed his cheek, snatched up her bouquet and raced up the path to the cabin. When she glanced back over her shoulder at him, John knew he'd made the right choice. Keeva was meant to be his, and he was meant to be hers.

Forever.

Chapter Eleven

"Stop fussing, Mam! If you don't leave me be, I'll miss my own wedding." Keeva frowned at her mother's image in the mirror as the woman tucked a curl in here and adjusted a flower there.

Keeva's hair was piled on her head with tiny little pink rosebuds pinned into the curls. She wore a beautiful peacock blue dress her sister had made for her. A matching velvet waistcoat with pink embroidered roses gave the gown an elegant air, along with the yards and yards of light blue and dark blue velvet ribbon stitched in rows along the hem of the skirt and the knee-length jacket that went over the ensemble.

"Do not tell your sisters, because I'll deny it if you do, but you are the most beautiful bride I've ever seen, my darling girl." Eira gave her a tight hug, kissed both cheeks, then stood back with tears in her eyes. "I can hardly believe my baby is getting married. It seems like just yesterday I was rocking you to sleep."

"I know, Mam, but I'm all grown up, and hopefully someday I'll have a sweet baby of my own to rock to sleep and sing her the lullabies you sang to me."

"Oh, wouldn't that be lovely," Eira said, clasping her hands beneath her chin. "You truly are a vision, Keeva. John won't know what to think when he sees you."

Keeva grinned, thinking of John's reaction to her gown, then picked up the bouquet of pink roses Nan Nichols had put together for her. She sniffed the blooms and felt tears welling in her eyes. Not because she was sad or afraid to marry the man of her dreams, but because she was so ridiculously happy.

"No tears, darling. Just happy smiles." Eira brushed a drop from Keeva's cheek. She gave her one more hug and then stepped back with a knowing look. "I'm so glad you waited a month to marry since it gave us time to be here with you. It's wonderful some of John's family could travel all the way from Maine to join in celebrating your nuptials."

"His parents have welcomed me into their family, but I really feel connected to his brother Mark, and his wife. Did you know John and Lisbeth have been friends since their young school days?"

"I believe I heard John and Mark sharing that with Evan last night at supper."

Keeva smiled, thinking of the big, boisterous group that had gathered for a meal at the hotel the previous evening. Evan had made arrangements ahead of time with Edith, and she'd been most accommodating, sliding tables together so they could all eat like one big family, which is exactly what Keeva felt they were.

A family.

Hers and his, and what she hoped would one day be theirs.

There had been moments in the last month that she'd felt the need to pinch herself to make sure she wasn't dreaming, but John assured her he was real. Their love was real. The future they'd create together was as real as the beating of their hearts.

He'd spoken last Sunday about dreams, and dreaming with faith. Keeva knew he'd spoken the words just for her to hear. She had dreamed of John for so long, and now they were to be wed. It was a dream that still seemed impossible, but a glance at her mother's beaming face confirmed it was about to happen.

"I hope you have a wonderfully happy life, my darling," Eira said, giving Keeva one last hug. "Come, now. It's time." She opened the door, kissed her husband's cheek, and went upstairs to take her seat in the front pew of the church.

Keeva had gotten ready in one of the basement rooms of the church she'd recently cleaned and organized. She smiled at her father as he held out an arm to her.

"You are every bit as lovely as your mother on our wedding day," Hiram said, giving her a warm, affectionate smile. "Are you sure you want to marry a pastor, baby girl? You'll never be rich, and there are times life will likely be quite hard."

"I've already learned life is hard for everyone from time to time. You just have to walk in faith to make it through. Besides, I will be rich in the most important things, Dad. I'll live in a home full of love, with a man who serves God. What better thing could I possibly ask for or need?"

"Nothing, Keeva. Not a thing." Her father kissed her temple as they reached the top of the steps, then Henley signaled for the piano player to begin the song to which Keeva would walk down the aisle.

She had no idea the church was packed to overflowing, or who filled the pews and stood pressed shoulder to shoulder in the back. All she knew was that John was waiting for her in a new suit that was a gift from his parents, smiling at her with love in his eyes. He'd asked Pastor Eagon from Baker City to perform the ceremony for them, and it added to the specialness of the day to be joined in holy matrimony by one of John's friends in the church where they would serve as long as the Lord guided them to remain in Holiday.

When Hiram handed Keeva's hand to John, she felt a little burst of heat shoot up her arm and knew John felt the same from the spark that snapped in his striking blue eyes.

He looked beyond handsome in the suit. She grinned when she realized instead of his perfectly parted, smoothed hair, he'd worn it tousled in the casual style she liked best. They'd already begun to mesh their lives together in a way that would bind their hearts for the remainder of their days on earth.

Pastor Eagon greeted everyone and began the ceremony. Dillon Durant stood up with John, and Henley stood with Keeva.

After they exchanged vows, John slid an exquisite gold band with an oval diamond onto her finger. It fit like it was made for her, even though she knew the ring had belonged to his grandmother. She was honored to wear it and hoped she and John would have a rich, full life of service to God, caring for others, and loving one another just as his grandparents had done.

"You may kiss your bride," Pastor Eagon said with a broad smile, and John wasted no time in bracketing Keeva's face, then giving her a sweet, reverent kiss. Before she could pull away, he kissed the tip of her nose and winked at her. His way of promising more ardent kisses to come.

A few hours later, after they'd enjoyed cake and punch with their family and friends and what seemed like most of the town, John helped Keeva into a buggy borrowed from R.C.

They would spend the next five days up at Evan and Henley's cabin before they returned to Holiday and a new routine of life there.

Keeva still intended to sell baked goods to Edith Piedmont when she wasn't cooking, cleaning, and helping John at the church. Life would be busy and full.

But best of all, it would be filled with love.

"Are you ready?" John asked as he slid onto the buggy seat beside her and lifted the reins.

"More than ready," Keeva said, wrapping her hands around John's arm and leaning her head against his shoulder. "I'm so glad you stepped out in faith to follow your heart, John."

"I had to, since those steps led straight to you."

She kissed his cheek, then waved as she tossed her bouquet into the crowd gathered around them. Unable to see who caught it, she smiled as people clapped and cheered, then shifted her attention back to her husband.

"I have no idea what tomorrow will bring," she said as John snapped the lines and the horse started down the street, into their future. "But I do know how very blessed I am to share it with you."

Keep reading for a preview of Rowan Reed's journey to a happily ever after.

Keeva's Cottage Pie

Here's the recipe for Keeva's delicious cottage pie! It is a comfort meal that is so tasty!

For the Cottage Pie
2 pounds lean ground beef
1 tablespoon minced onion
1 cup diced carrots
1 cup diced celery
1 tablespoon minced garlic
2 ½ cups beef broth
2 tablespoons Worcestershire sauce
2 sprigs fresh thyme
2 bay leaves
prepared mashed potatoes

For the Mashed Potatoes
3 pounds peeled and diced Yukon gold potatoes
1 teaspoon olive oil
½ cup milk
2 tablespoons butter
½ cup shredded cheddar cheese
½ teaspoon ground nutmeg

Directions:
For the Cottage Pie
In a large skillet, brown the ground beef until no longer pink, then add the onion, carrots, celery, and garlic.
Preheat oven to 350 degrees F.

Allow the vegetables to soften for three minutes, then add the broth, Worcestershire sauce, thyme, and bay leaves. Stir to combine, and allow to cook over medium heat until most of the liquid has been absorbed, approximately twenty minutes.

Remove the thyme and bay leaves and then spoon the meat mixture into an oven safe 9x13 casserole dish. Top with prepared mashed potatoes.

Bake for 30 minutes until golden brown.

For the Mashed Potatoes

Add the potatoes to a large pot along with olive oil and fill with cold water. Bring to a boil and allow to cook until the potatoes have softened, about fifteen minutes. The oil helps keep the potatoes from boiling over.

Drain the potatoes, put them back in the pot, and add the milk, butter, cheese, and nutmeg. Mash with an electric mixer to get a creamy mashed potato or a hand masher for a chunkier version.

Author's Note

Thank you for reading John and Keeva's story. They certainly seem like an unlikely couple, don't they? But it's wonderful how things work out when we just continue onward in faith.

I always feel so encouraged when I think about the word faith and all it means to me. I hope dreaming with faith is something that will bring you contentment and joy.

When I was working on ideas for the opening scene for this story, we ended up discussing it at the dinner table one evening. My nephew, who is living with us while he attends college, suggested having Keeva drape her scarf over something as a challenge to the boys who wished to court her. A corner post of a fence seemed ideal. So, thank you, Will, for sparking the idea!

Years ago, when I was in college, my grandmother gave me an old hymnal that I think might have even been her mother's hymnal. My dad has it now, but when we go to visit, I sure enjoy looking through it, and reading the notes written on the pages.

When I was trying to decide the hymns to include in the story, I happened upon an 1885 hymnal online that not only listed the hymns, but also had images of the pages. It was so wonderful to flip through them and see those old familiar hymns. "God Be with You Till We Meet Again" always makes me think of my grandma.

The scene at Elk Creek Ranch where the group gathered around the table discussing missionaries to

China comes from an old newspaper article from April of 1886. It mentioned a great need for missionaries. I like to find newspapers that correspond to the timeline of my books because I love to imagine the characters reading the paper and consider which topics might have stood out enough for them to discuss.

The joke R.C. told was also in a newspaper under a column titled "humor."

The potato patties Keeva fixed is a nod to the patties my mom used to occasionally make if we had leftover mashed potatoes (which rarely happened). She mixed the potatoes with eggs and some seasoning and fried them until the outside was crispy, golden, and so delicious. I wish I'd asked her to write down the recipe for me.

Speaking of my mom, she liked to use home remedies whenever possible. Once, when I was about fourteen, I had a spot on my index finger that wouldn't go away. She dredged up some old wives' tale, and tried to convince me it would work. She soaked raw meat in vinegar (usually a piece of steak), then placed a little piece over the spot wrapped with waterproof medical tape overnight.

I hated it!

It stunk, and it was so disgusting to have that thing taped to my finger all night. After several weeks and the spot not disappearing, a trip to the doctor was necessary.

So, that's where the inspiration for Keeva's "quackery" came from.

A special thanks to Katrina, Allison, Alice, Linda, and my Hopeless Romantics team for all your help with John and Keeva's story.

Thank you, dear reader, for going on another Holiday adventure. Be sure to look for *Dreams for Courage*, the next story in this series.

Keep dreaming with faith, my friends!

Shanna

Preview Dreams For Courage

March 1886
Chicago

Leaning heavily on a crooked stick that served as a cane, Rhetta Wallace took another shuffling step forward, adjusting the basket she carried higher on her arm. Soot streaked her cheeks, and frizzy gray hair peeked from beneath a tattered rag she'd tied on her head. Back bent and eyes squinting against the bright morning light, she smiled at a stranger passing by, revealing the blackened hole where front teeth should have resided.

"Psst! Rhetta. Psst!"

Rhetta pretended not to hear anything as she neared an alley. With slow, measured steps, she backed herself up to an upturned keg and settled her girth on the makeshift seat.

"What is it, Lee?" she asked, barely moving her lips as she turned ever so slightly toward the dark shadows of the alley.

"There's a man at your office. He wouldn't leave and told me I had to come fetch you."

"Name?" Rhetta asked, taking a long straw from her basket and sticking it in her mouth, pretending to chew on it.

"Said he represents Senator Tomlinson."

Rhetta almost choked on the straw and spit it out. Without looking behind her, she stood. "I'll be there as soon as I can. Give him tea and cookies."

"Will do."

From experience, Rhetta knew Leland Turner, her assistant and unofficial ward, would disappear into the shadows and return quickly to her office.

Rhetta continued down the street, keeping a steady eye on the man she was following. He turned at the corner, walked a few blocks to a residential area, and knocked on the door of a small home in need of paint and repair.

The door swung open, and a lovely young woman launched herself into the man's arms. He kissed her soundly, lifted her in his arms, and continued kissing her as he walked into the house and toed the door shut behind him.

Rhetta sighed, disappointed she'd been correct in assuming the worst. The irate wife who hired Rhetta to see if her husband was the philandering lout she'd determined him to be was going to be even more livid by news of this recent encounter.

Three times in the past two weeks, Rhetta had trailed the man to bawdy houses. Four days ago, he'd had a suspicious meeting in the park with a woman who'd appeared half his age. Notes were passed, and Rhetta could only guess it was information about a liaison.

Like this one.

She wrote down the address of the house and a few key notes on a writing tablet she took from the basket she carried, then stepped behind the nearest building, took off the rag and wig from her head and the shawl that looked like a dog had chewed it beyond redemption, stuffing them into her basket.

Casting away the stick she'd used for a cane, she wiped her cheeks on her dress sleeve, then walked to the corner and hailed a hansom cab. At her dirty, worn attire, he demanded payment before he'd take her to her office.

"Fine," she said, slapping a coin onto his palm with a huff. Rhetta sat back on the leather seat of the conveyance and reviewed what little detail she knew about Senator Tomlinson. The man was from Cincinnati. She wondered how he'd acquired her name since she lived in Chicago and had all her life. Then again, she had a string of wealthy clients who were good at passing along her name in referrals.

Rhetta generally hated the cases they hired her to pursue, like the wife who wanted evidence of her husband's wandering ways. But Rhetta took those jobs and charged outrageous fees, which allowed her to take on cases that mattered for the poor and underprivileged who had no way to pay. At the end of the day, she felt one thing balanced the other and allowed her to rest peacefully. Or as peacefully as a woman who has spent the past eleven years working as a private detective could.

"Thank you," Rhetta said with cool politeness when the driver stopped as she'd directed, around the corner from the front door of her second-floor office. She rented the space above a photographer's studio. The photographer happened to be her cousin, so she was watched over by James although he had learned to mind his own business and not raise his eyebrows too high when she traipsed by his windows wearing one of her outlandish costumes.

Most of the time if she was in costume, Rhetta used the stairs located in the alley and entered through her back door. In a rush, she hopped out of the cab and raced around the corner into the alley, then took the stairs two at a time.

Rhetta jammed her key into the lock on her back door and swung the portal open, stepping into the hallway. She went directly into her costume room and found Lee had left a steaming pitcher of water for her to use to wash up.

"Bless that boy," Rhetta whispered to herself as she scrubbed her hands and face, removed the pins holding her hair close to her scalp, and combed out her long brown tresses. As she looked in the mirror and quickly styled her wavy hair into a loose coil she fastened at the back of her head, she surveyed her features.

Except for her bright blue eyes, Rhetta didn't think there was anything remarkable or even very memorable about her appearance. Her nose wasn't too long or too short. Her face not too round or oblong. Her chin could be a little on the stubborn side, but she had lips that weren't too puffy or too thin.

Overall, she felt average, which worked well when she wanted to blend in with a crowd. Not quite as well for attracting a suitor although Rhetta was not looking.

Men found her too bold, opinionated, and determined for their liking. After the number of unfaithful husbands she'd been hired to follow, she wasn't convinced a faithful one existed among the male species.

With flying fingers, she unbuttoned the ragged dress, removed the padding she'd fastened around her middle, and tossed off a petticoat fashioned from an old bed sheet.

She yanked on a lace-trimmed petticoat, pulled on her skirt and shirtwaist, then added a jacket that gave her a polished, professional appearance. The pink ensemble, edged in black, was striking and elegant, and a gift from one of Rhetta's clients. In fact, Mrs. Brown had been most generous in giving Rhetta five expensive outfits Mrs. Brown had no longer been able to wear after giving birth to twins two years ago.

Mr. Brown had been one of the exceptions to Rhetta's rule that all men were detestable brutes. She'd followed him almost daily for a month and discovered the reason he kept secrets from his wife was to plan a surprise party for her birthday. Once Rhetta relayed that happy news, the woman had been elated and paid Rhetta's fee with a bonus, as well as offering the clothes that Rhetta had been thrilled to receive.

With a slight tug to the hem of the jacket to adjust it, Rhetta touched a bit of her favorite perfume to both wrists. Regardless of her career, a woman needed to feel feminine, at least to Rhetta's way of thinking.

She breezed from the room and down the hallway toward the entry area, where Lee had his own desk. He kept anyone from storming any further into the office without his approval and was there to receive visitors.

Years ago, she'd been watching the sale of ill-gotten goods in a seedy neighborhood when she caught a little boy trying to pick her pocket. Rhetta had grabbed him by the seat of the pants when he'd tried to run off and peppered him with enough questions he finally burst into tears and confessed he had no home and couldn't recall his parents or if he had any siblings. He'd been living on the streets as long as he could remember.

Rhetta had taken him home and fed him, cleaned him up, and given him a place to sleep. In the morning he'd been gone, but he'd returned a few days later, starving, and sporting a black eye. As he'd wolfed down a bowl of hearty beef stew, she'd made him a bargain. If he stayed, she'd keep him fed, give him a warm bed, and never hit him if he in turn agreed not to leave without telling her where he was heading, refrained from stealing from her, bathed with some regularity, and would work as her assistant.

DREAMS WITH FAITH

He'd shaken her hand in agreement, and Lee had been with her since. Neither of them knew his real birthday, so they chose the day she'd first encountered him as his birthday. Rhetta had guessed him to be around six, and Lee had just turned fourteen two weeks ago.

As a private investigator, Rhetta had done everything she could to unearth Leland's identity and some record of his existence, but it was as if he'd fallen from the sky and landed in Chicago's slums.

Regardless, she had made inquiries about adopting him. It seemed a judge would rather a boy live homeless and alone than allow a single woman perfectly capable of providing a stable home to adopt him. So, despite the lack of legalities, Rhetta considered Lee her son. Likely the only one she'd ever have since she would turn twenty-nine in April.

According to the whispers she occasionally overheard from people who liked to gossip, she was an old maid too contrary and odd to ever catch a man.

Rhetta wasn't contrary or an old maid, at least to her way of thinking. Besides, she had no time for putting up with the demands of a husband when she had a boy who needed her and work that fulfilled her. The bit about her being odd ... well, that was perhaps disputable. She had always felt different from the other girls her age. She'd never been content to sit at home sewing samplers. Not when her father had encouraged her to dream big dreams and follow an adventurous path.

Rhetta stepped into the reception area and glanced at the dour-faced man seated on a chair in the corner. She looked at Lee, and he shrugged. With a smile plastered on her face, she took a step toward the man, extending her hand in greeting. "Hello, Mister …"

"Reynolds," Lee whispered in her ear, handing her a fresh writing tablet and pencil.

The man ignored her outstretched hand, so she withdrew it.

"Welcome, Mr. Reynolds," she said, forcing herself to maintain a smile. "How may I be of service to you today?"

The man stood and gave her a long, narrowed-gaze study. "You kept me waiting long enough, Miss Wallace. However, Senator Tomlinson is determined to speak with you about a delicate matter."

Rhetta had no notion as to what *delicate matter* the senator wanted to discuss, but she had an idea it was one she wouldn't like. Was his wife still alive? She couldn't recall. Whatever he sought her assistance with would likely be something scandalous and ridiculous, but she'd take the case because she had several clients unable to pay who truly needed her assistance.

"Is the senator in town?" Rhetta asked, meeting the man's stare with a frosty glare of her own. She refused to be cowed by him, especially in her own office.

"No. He's willing to pay your travel expenses if you could meet him next Tuesday."

"I will meet with him, but I make no promises other than arriving on time."

"Very well." The man took a thick envelope from the pocket of his coat and handed it to her. "All the information you'll need for the trip is in there." He tipped his head to her and left without another word.

Rhetta sank onto an overstuffed chair and looked at Lee. He stretched his arms above his head, leaned back slightly, and then grabbed the lapels of the vest he wore as he lowered his voice. "I'm Mister Mighty Britches, come to toss out demands from a corrupt politician. You will listen and obey me, little woman."

A chuckle rolled out of her before she could rein it in. Lee was forever doing impersonations, most of them quite well, and making her laugh.

"Sit down, you rascal, and let's see what Senator Tomlinson has to say."

Rhetta opened the envelope to find two train tickets, reservations for two rooms at one of the city's finest hotels, and a map with details for meeting the senator at a park near the hotel. It seemed she was welcome to bring Lee if she chose. The fact that the senator knew about Lee bothered her. Had he hired someone to spy on them? Someone like Mr. Reynolds?

A shiver slid over her spine at the thought of anyone watching them. Despite her aversion to this case and the senator, she decided she'd at least hear him out.

It looked like she and Lee were about to go on a short journey.

"I get to go?" Lee asked, reading the note she passed to him.

"Yes, you do. We'll pack tomorrow after we return from the church service and lunch with the cousins. The tickets appear to be for the afternoon train Monday, but I'll see if we can switch to a morning departure. I want time to visit the park and get a better idea of the area where we'll be staying."

"What can I do to help?"

"Make sure my satchel is packed with fresh supplies. We'll need tablets, pencils, and contracts in the event I decide to take this case." She handed him the unused writing tablet and pencil. "You are in charge of bringing snacks."

Lee grinned. The past few months, he seemed to have two hollow legs. The only time he didn't complain about being hungry was when he was sleeping. Rhetta had always kept fruit and cookies at the office for him to snack on after school and on the weekends if he accompanied her there. Now, she had whole loaves of bread, dried strips of beef, and tins of crackers, as well as fruit and cookies.

Thankfully, there was a bakery across the street and a café just around the corner if he ate all of the food in the office before she could replenish it.

"I'll make sure we have plenty of snacks. Is there a trunk I can pack them in?"

Rhetta gave him a playful nudge, knowing he was teasing. She rose and gathered the contents of the envelope Mr. Reynolds had left, tucked them inside, then walked into her office.

She wrote a letter to the wife of the cheating husband, sealed it in an envelope, and sent Lee to deliver it, then made her way to the train depot to see about switching their tickets.

Although she dreaded meeting the senator, part of her was excited about embarking on a new adventure.

Available on Amazon

Thank You

Thank you for reading *Dreams of Love*.
If you enjoyed the story, I'd be so grateful if you would leave a review. It's a great way for readers to discover new-to-them authors!

Be sure you check out all the books in the Holiday Dreams series!

More Sweet Romances

*If you love historical romances,
I hope you'll take a look at these sweet and wholesome series!*

Pendleton Petticoats Series

Set in the western town of Pendleton, Oregon at the turn of the 20th century, each book in this series bears the name of the heroine, all brave yet very different.
Begin with *Aundy*, or the *Pendleton Petticoats* boxed set!

Baker City Brides Series

Determined women, strong men and a town known as the Denver of the Blue Mountains takes center stage in these novels set during its days of gold in the 1890s.

The *Regional Romance Series* features books with three connected sweet romances.
Discover how one matchmaker ends up traveling to Oregon to set one reluctant groom on his ear in *Grass Valley Brides*.
And read about a romantic rancher who will do anything to avoid falling in love in *Romance at Rinehart's Crossing*.

About the Author

PHOTO BY SHANA BAILEY PHOTOGRAPHY

USA Today bestselling author Shanna Hatfield is a farm girl who loves to write. Her sweet historical and contemporary romances are filled with sarcasm, humor, hope, and hunky heroes.

When Shanna isn't dreaming up unforgettable characters, twisting plots, or covertly seeking dark, decadent chocolate, she hangs out with her beloved husband, Captain Cavedweller, at their home in the Pacific Northwest.

Shanna loves to hear from readers.
Connect with her online:
Website: shannahatfield.com
Email: shanna@shannahatfield.com

Printed in Great Britain
by Amazon